## "We should call the police.

"We can tell them what happened at your cabin yesterday, and you can tell them about when I got shot. This whole thing can be over right now."

Casey took a step back, her eyes wide and fearful. "I can't do that, Jack." What was it that had her so scared?

A flash of frustration filled him. "Can't, or won't?"

"Both. It's the same thing."

Jack noticed that she didn't deny she'd seen the shooting. She was just refusing to testify, and without her testimony, Jack still had nothing concrete to prove his innocence or Stevens's guilt.

He glanced back up at Casey, who had taken another step backward. She looked incredibly vulnerable and her expression squeezed his heart. He still didn't know her story, but she had just saved his life. Again. Jack made a decision. He would figure out her history and the cause of her reticence at some point, but for now he'd have to think of something else.

**Books by Kathleen Tailer**

Love Inspired Suspense

*Under the Marshal's Protection*
*The Reluctant Witness*

## KATHLEEN TAILER

is an attorney who works for the Supreme Court of Florida in the Office of the State Courts Administrator, where she works on programs that are designed to enhance and improve dependency courts throughout the state. She previously worked for the Florida Department of Children and Families, handling child-abuse cases both as a line attorney and in the DCF General Counsel's Office. She enjoys teaching business law online classes at Liberty University and working on finding homes for orphans with the Open Door Adoption Agency. She and her husband have eight children, five of whom they adopted. When not in the office, Kathleen spends most of her time cheering for her kids at different events or spending quiet time (hah!) at home. Kathleen has previously published two articles for *Fostering Families Today,* a magazine for foster families, and two novels, entitled *Children in the Wind* and *Under the Marshal's Protection.* She also plays drums on the worship team at Calvary Chapel Thomasville.

# THE RELUCTANT WITNESS

## KATHLEEN TAILER

**HARLEQUIN**® LOVE INSPIRED® SUSPENSE

Recycling programs for this product may not exist in your area.

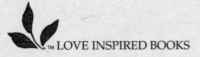

™ LOVE INSPIRED BOOKS

ISBN-13: 978-0-373-67579-1

THE RELUCTANT WITNESS

Copyright © 2013 by Kathleen Tailer

All rights reserved. Except for use in any review, the reproduction or utilization of this work in whole or in part in any form by any electronic, mechanical or other means, now known or hereafter invented, including xerography, photocopying and recording, or in any information storage or retrieval system, is forbidden without the written permission of the editorial office, Love Inspired Books, 233 Broadway, New York, NY 10279 U.S.A.

This is a work of fiction. Names, characters, places and incidents are either the product of the author's imagination or are used fictitiously, and any resemblance to actual persons, living or dead, business establishments, events or locales is entirely coincidental.

This edition published by arrangement with Love Inspired Books.

® and TM are trademarks of Love Inspired Books, used under license. Trademarks indicated with ® are registered in the United States Patent and Trademark Office, the Canadian Trade Marks Office and in other countries.

www.Harlequin.com

**Printed in U.S.A.**

Greater love has no one than this,
that someone lay down his life for his friends.
—*John* 15:13

For my dear friends Wendy Maxwell Franchell, Suzy Harrington and Linda Merritt. Some friendships fade over time, but in you, I've found friendship that will last a lifetime. May God bless each of you with a full and happy life.

# ONE

The first bullet whizzed by his head and ricocheted off the rock behind him. The second caught him square in the shoulder and burned like fire immediately upon impact. Pain shot down his arm, and he could feel the blood dampening his shirt as it pooled around the wound.

FBI agent Jack Mitchell took a fortifying breath, then cast a quick look around the tree and returned fire. A shootout was the last thing he'd expected when he'd come to the isolated cabin looking for a lead in his current case. But while he hadn't been expecting the gunmen, they had clearly been expecting him.

As best he could tell, there were at least two men out there shooting at him. He fired again and heard a moan as one of his bullets struck home, eliminating one of his enemies. He took cover again behind the tree and patted his pocket to assess his ammunition stock. He still had one full clip of fifteen cartridges left. He hoped it was enough. The remaining gunman was still shooting at him, and bits of bark and leaves flew like fireworks as the bullets decimated the surrounding forest.

The shooting stopped abruptly, and Jack guessed that his opponent was reloading or changing his position. He looked quickly around the tree and saw no movement, but he knew the remaining shooter was still out there somewhere. He bent and looked carefully around the surrounding area. It was time for him to move, too—he just needed to decide which direction was safest. He grimaced as pain from his shoulder intensified and he shifted to ease the throbbing. With a short prayer, he headed up toward a boulder to his right.

He never made it.

Another bullet caught him in the thigh and he fell hard, way short of his destination. He struggled to stand again and make it to cover as agonizing pain radiated through his leg, but he could barely do more than shift himself forward. The pain on its own was nearly debilitating, and it didn't help that he was losing blood fast.

Suddenly he heard a noise from directly in

front of him and realized there was a weapon pointed straight at his chest. He glanced up to lock eyes with the man holding the gun and saw a coldness there that chilled him right to the bone. He'd known Brett Stevens since they'd gone to the academy together. They had been partners for almost five years, yet he had never suspected the man of being dirty. Stevens had hid it well. And the gun he held on Jack with no hint of regret made it clear that he planned to hide it awhile longer.

Dread washed over him. He was going to die, right here on the forest floor. Regrets flashed through his head. He wasn't ready to die. He was only thirty years old, and the rising star in the Bureau's local field office. There were still plenty of things he was planning to do with his life. Apparently, he wasn't going to get the chance.

"You shouldn't have come out here, Mitchell," Stevens said, his voice grating like gravel. "Put your gun down now."

Another gunman joined them in the clearing and Jack realized that there had been more men out in the woods than he had originally thought. With three guns against him he had been outmaneuvered from the beginning. He glanced at the new man, but once he realized that the guy was a stranger, Jack ignored him and focused on Stevens. Maybe he had a chance of convincing his partner that murder wasn't the answer.

"This can all be worked out, Brett. If you give yourself up now, we can still fix this. Don't throw your life away."

"My life? My life has been over ever since my team lost the Super Bowl. I have debts, Jack. Colby offered me a chance to make the cash to pay what I owe. It was all working out just fine… until you decided to start digging. You brought this on yourself." He motioned slightly with his gun, then brought it back to point at Jack's midriff. "Besides, Jack, out of all the lives out here, the one you should be worried about is your own."

"Don't do this," Jack said, shaking his head, his hands up in a motion of surrender. "I'll help you get back on the right track. I'll do whatever it takes."

Stevens laughed, but it was filled with bitterness. "Nobody can help me. I'm too far down the road to turn back now." He motioned with his pistol again. "What's in the bag?"

Jack glanced down at the satchel he had dropped on the ground. He had found a laptop and quite a few papers in the private investigator's cabin that he had just searched, but he needed time to analyze everything before he would know the true value of what he had discovered.

Earlier he'd hoped the laptop and papers would contain the evidence he had been hunting for that would implicate a ring of conspirators operating out of the federal courthouse. Apparently Stevens was also one of the conspirators. The knowledge was a bitter pill for Jack to swallow. He had considered that maybe someone on the FBI payroll was involved, but it had never occurred to him that Stevens would turn on his own. How had he missed that? Why hadn't he seen the evil lurking right below the surface in this man he had worked with every day for the past five years?

He glanced up at Stevens, whose familiar eyes now looked dark and sinister. "Just a laptop and some papers," Jack hedged, hoping that if he somehow survived this encounter he could still use the evidence to break the case.

Stevens aimed and shook his head. "Goodbye, Mitchell."

Jack tried to dive behind a tree to escape, but it was an exercise in futility. The impact from the bullet caught him hard and spun his body around as it ripped into the flesh on his side. He was still falling when the second shot caught him in the head. For the moment, gravity had saved his life, giving him enough momentum that the bullet sliced a trail across his forehead rather than passing straight through to his brain. But how long would it take before blood loss—or another bullet from Stevens—finished the job?

His body hit the ground hard. Pain enveloped him and he struggled to stay conscious. He felt Stevens kick his ribs, but he had enough presence of mind to try to remain as still as possible. He felt another kick, and it took everything inside him not to react to the agony that radiated up his side and around the assortment of bullet wounds. He heard the other man take a few steps toward him and holster his weapon.

"Now what? This partner of yours was a pretty good shot. He managed to kill Milo down on the ridge. Now we've got two bodies to dispose of."

"Let's take care of Milo's body first." Stevens shifted and Jack could hear his partner's shoes rustling the leaves as he started to pace.

His partner had always had a creative side. Jack guessed Stevens was already devising a plan in his mind to explain what had happened this afternoon. The man would probably tell just enough truth to keep him from mixing up the story if he ever got interrogated, but he would name Jack as the criminal and would try to get the conspiracy investigation closed as soon as possible. The thought made Jack sick inside.

A moment passed, then another. Suddenly Stevens stopped and a laugh erupted.

"What's so funny?" the other gunman snarled, his voice gruff. "I don't see anything to laugh about in two dead bodies that might somehow come back and bite me."

Stevens secured his weapon and snapped the holster shut. "Let's put Milo in Jack's trunk and park his car back at his apartment. It'll throw the local cops off our trail, and Jack won't be around to defend himself or point the finger at us. That should keep the heat off and make such a huge stink that nobody will even think to look in our direction. After we dump Milo, we can come back up here, clean up the scene and bury Jack. My uncle has some property near here that'll be the perfect place to hide the body. Nobody ever goes over there."

"You're the boss. I've got some plastic in my trunk for just such an occasion. We can make it look like he was about to dispose of the body but got interrupted."

"Perfect."

A wave of nausea swept over Jack as he fought to keep in the here and now. Still, he struggled through the pain and tried to concentrate on their words. He heard Stevens reach down, grab the satchel and sift through the contents. A few seconds passed and then the bag closed with a snap.

"See anything in there that's a problem?"

"I don't know. It's going to take me some time to sort through it all. I'll take it along just in case."

Jack tried not to tense as he felt Stevens reach over, pat his pockets and pull out his car keys.

"Aren't you even gonna check the guy's pulse? There's an awful lot of blood, but I'm telling you I don't want to take any chances."

Stevens's voice took on a menacing tone. "Relax. You worry too much. I know killing Jack wasn't part of the plan, but I think it can actually work to our advantage if we play our cards right." He paused. "All right. If it makes you feel better, I'll check." Jack felt Stevens reach toward his neck, but suddenly a cell phone ring broke the silence.

Stevens pulled back and answered the phone. "What? Okay. I'm on my way. Don't move without me." The cell phone snapped shut with a click and Stevens stood abruptly.

"We have to go. Now. Colby has an emergency and needs us downtown. Let's get Milo's body and get out of here. We'll come back and take care of Jack later."

Jack heard them retreat and breathed a sigh of relief. He was alive—for now. But his thoughts were getting fuzzy and he could feel the life ebbing from him as his blood soaked into the ground. He tried to move and groaned as another wave of pain swept over him. He paused a moment, then tried again. His limbs felt heavy and nothing seemed to work right. With another groan he succumbed to the blackness, wondering if he would ever see the light of day again.

Casey Johnson gasped and shrank back against the bushes. From her position on the cliff she had clearly seen the entire scene play out, and her heart was beating overtime as fear washed over her. They had just killed that man in cold blood!

She'd been out taking her daily run when she'd heard the first shot and had quickly made her way toward the edge of the cliff to see the valley below. Seconds later she had crouched behind some shrubbery, hoping the plant and her green shirt would camouflage her from the murderers' sight as the horrible scene had played out in front of her. What were they doing up here? Why had they killed that man? Her heart felt as if it was about to come right out of her chest and her limbs felt frozen and numb.

A movement caught her eye and she saw the two men get into a blue two-door vehicle, drive down the road a short distance and pull onto the grass before exiting the car again. A few seconds later the two men returned, carrying a body out of the woods. Casey swallowed hard as realization swept over her. Two men were dead, not just one. She watched, horrified, as they wrapped the body in a large sheet of plastic and threw it into the trunk of the car. Seconds later, the blue car and a brown sedan, each driven by one of the shooters, sped down the road, leaving a plume of dirt and a dead man behind them.

Questions and trepidation spun through Casey's head. What had happened? Why had there been a gun battle out here only a short distance from her cabin? She sat back and tried to keep her hands from shaking. Did the gunshots have anything to do with her situation? Various scenarios abounded in her mind, and she stayed hidden a few moments, mulling over the possibilities. She'd thought she was still safe, but she should have known better than to have assumed anything. Still, the idea that her brother-in-law had sent them didn't quite fit. If the men had been looking for her, they wouldn't have ended up shooting each other, or left so quickly without finding their quarry. No, it seemed clear that their target had been the man that was still lying on the ground below.

She quickly raced down the mountainside, anxious to see if the man who had been left on the forest floor was indeed dead or had somehow survived. Even as she approached, two questions rang through her head. Why hadn't the murderers taken his body, as well? Would they be back? She'd seen the men talking from her spot on the ridge but she hadn't been able to overhear their words, so she couldn't be sure about their plans.

Nothing about this scenario made sense. They were pretty high up in the mountains, and it was rare for Casey to have any human company other than her niece, who lived with her. Only a few cabins dotted the mountainside, and most were empty except during the summer months. She had picked this location for that very reason. She didn't want any visitors. In fact, keeping her location a secret was vital. Still, she couldn't just walk away without at least checking on the fallen man.

She tripped on a root but righted herself

quickly and continued down the mountain, slowing her pace to make sure she didn't reveal her presence in case there were others still in the woods. It didn't take long for her to find a blood trail, and she gasped at the red stains that painted the ground. Surely the man was dead, or there wouldn't have been so much blood. She followed it back to where it had probably started with the man's first injury, before the final confrontation. A large pool of blood had soaked into the ground, and even more droplets of blood painted the leaves of the nearby bushes. She looked around carefully, searching for any other clues that might explain what had happened and why the men were in the woods in the first place, but she found nothing.

"Help me." The voice was soft, so soft that at first, Casey thought she'd imagined it. She quickly headed up to where she had seen the shooting and heard a soft moan as she approached. She stepped over a fallen log, her eyes warily searching the area around her. She heard another moan and moved cautiously toward the sound, constantly looking over her shoulder, just in case.

The man was lying on his back, but Casey could see drag marks on the ground where he had tried to push himself up. Blood stained his khaki pants and the navy long-sleeved shirt he was wearing. She stepped closer and got a better look at the embroidery on the shirt pocket. There was a law enforcement shield with the words Federal Bureau of Investigation written underneath.

She flinched and felt her heart skip a beat. FBI? This could be a disaster! Fear flooded her as she thought of her peaceful mountain retreat invaded by federal agents. How could she protect herself from that? How could she protect Chloe? Her legs tensed and every instinct in her told her to run.

But she wouldn't. She'd stay calm and think this through. The man was alone for now, and certainly no threat to her in his condition. And she wouldn't be able to live with herself if she just left him behind without even trying to help.

She looked at his face and gasped. A large gash ripped the skin just below the hairline over his left eye, and blood covered his face. Head wounds always bled an amazing amount, but this man's wounds made him look as if he were already dead.

She knelt carefully by his side and felt for a pulse. He groaned at her touch. That was good.

If he was alert enough to feel the pressure, then maybe he wasn't as far gone as she had thought. His heartbeat was strong and he seemed to be breathing well, but he had already lost a lot of blood. She began to pull back, but he grasped her arm.

"Help me," he whispered. His eyes were open but were so full of agony that Casey wasn't even sure that he was seeing her. She covered his hand with her own and squeezed it, then gently pulled her arm away from him, ignoring the blood.

"I'm going to help you. I promise." She examined the wound on his side and then gently felt underneath him to see if she could locate an exit wound. There was one, and she breathed a sigh of relief. Thankfully, the bullet had gone clean through. She did the same exam with the leg wound and found that that bullet had also left an exit wound. The man hadn't been so lucky with his shoulder wound and she knew that the bullet must still be in the muscle tissue. Quickly she pulled off her sweatshirt and started ripping it into strips, ignoring the cold that penetrated her thin T-shirt.

The man moved a little at her ministrations and groaned as she started binding his injuries. Casey started talking, trying to soothe him with her words as she worked. "It's okay, mister. I'm actually not a total novice at all of this. I was in med school for a few years and I'm trying to stop the bleeding for you. You're going to be okay. It's going to take you a while to heal, but you'll be fine once we stitch you up." She tried to infuse her voice with hope, but she knew that if she didn't get the bleeding stopped pretty quickly that he would die right here, lying on the ground.

Once she'd finished bandaging him, she took his face gently in her hands and tried to make eye contact with him. He had dark brown eyes that were full of anguish. She still wasn't sure if he was registering her presence or not, but she had to try.

"Look, you're too heavy for me to carry, and you're in no condition to walk out of here, so I need to go get my car. Stay put and I'll be right back, okay? Try not to move. I *will* come back. Do you hear me? I won't be long. I promise." She gave him a gentle smile, then turned and started running quickly toward her cabin. It was about a mile away and the adrenalin she was feeling helped her arrive at her front door in a little over fifteen minutes.

Chloe met her at the door, her eyes wide at the sight of the blood that had gotten all over Casey.

Mentally, Casey scolded herself for not having anticipated this problem. The child was only ten years old—of course she was spooked, especially with her own experiences with injuries.

"Aunt Casey? Oh, no, what happened? Are you okay?"

Casey nodded as she tried to catch her breath, quickly grabbing her car keys and heading to the bathroom as she did so. "It's not my blood, honey. I'm fine, but somebody else is hurt, and I need to go back and help him. Can you fill up a water bottle for me?" She grabbed several towels from under the sink, a bottle of hydrogen peroxide and a first-aid kit and raced toward the back door where the car was parked, then stopped and took the water bottle the girl held out to her.

"Chloe, I need your help. I'm going to bring the injured man back with me. Can you put some clean sheets on the couch? I'm also going to need your help bringing him into the house. He's gonna be really heavy."

Chloe nodded, her expression solemn. "Are you sure he's a nice man?" There was a measure of fear in her voice, so Casey stepped forward and carefully hugged her, trying to keep the majority of the blood from getting on the child as she did so.

"I hope so, Chloe. He was attacked by some bad men and he really needs our help. But you're right that we should be cautious around him. He's wearing a shirt that says he works for the FBI, so that makes him dangerous. We'll have to be very careful about how we talk around him. I have to go right now because every second counts if I want to help him, but we'll talk a lot more about this when I get him settled. Okay?" Casey gave her a squeeze, then raced to the car and started driving back down the mountain. Was she making a huge mistake? What if the man discovered her past? Time would tell....

# TWO

Jack had seen a princess. She had hovered over him for a few minutes and then disappeared, but he had definitely seen her. She looked exactly like the princess in the book his baby sister made him read to her over and over again when she was little. The funny thing was she wasn't wearing a gown or a tiara. Instead, her dark brown hair had been pulled back in a ponytail, and she was wearing a simple sweatshirt and running pants. Still, she had definitely had the most amazing blue eyes he had ever seen, and was the perfect twin to the beautiful princess from the storybook.

He wiped his eyes with his good hand, trying to get some of the blood away that was clouding his vision, but it seemed futile. The pain was so intense in so many places that he was still having trouble just staying conscious.

"Hey, mister. You still hanging in there?" The soft melodious voice surprised him, and when he opened his eyes, his princess was back, smiling at him and tying towels around the makeshift bandages that covered the wounds on his leg and torso. "I told you I'd be back. I promised—and I never break a promise."

His mouth didn't seem able to form words, so he just nodded, hoping she would understand. She moved his bad arm across his chest and somehow fashioned a sling around it that she tied to his neck. Then she put a washcloth against his head wound and secured it with an elastic bandage. Gently she wiped the blood out of his eyes with a small damp cloth, and he got a better look at her. She had a smile on her face that he assumed was for his benefit, but also a look of worry that she couldn't quite hide. After she finished her ministrations, she leaned over him and gently cupped his face again. As severely injured as he was, he still found himself mesmerized by her eyes.

"We have to move you now, and even though it's going to hurt, I'm gonna need your help. You're a big guy and I'm sure you're more than I can carry alone. Can you help me?"

Jack's mind raced as his brain came back online. Okay. She wasn't a princess after all, but she was helping him. He only remembered bits and pieces of what Stevens had said while standing over his body, but it was enough to know that he wasn't safe staying where he was. Cooperating with this stranger was his only chance of survival. He nodded to her and grimaced as she moved him slowly into a sitting position. She braced herself under his good shoulder and he did all he could to help, yet it was still slow going as she got him to his feet and moved him toward the car parked only a few feet away. Eventually they were able to maneuver him into the back seat, though small beads of sweat popped out on his forehead from the effort.

The next thing he knew, she was tugging at him again to help him get out of the car, and he realized that he must have blacked out during the journey. He looked around, searching for hospital attendants, but saw none. In fact, from what he could see, he was still in the woods near a small log cabin.

"Are we…hospital?" he asked quietly, struggling to make a complete thought.

"No, sorry. We're at my cabin. The nearest hospital is about two and a half hours away, and I doubt you could survive the trip."

A small girl suddenly appeared behind the woman, and he noticed she had the same big blue eyes. She was a pretty child, with blond hair instead of brown, yet her expression was marred with worry. As the woman pulled him up out of the car, the girl tried to offer assistance as well but finally gave up and awkwardly ended up holding the door open for them instead.

"Thanks, Chloe. You're the best." The woman's voice was soft, yet still somewhat musical to Jack's ears. That was the last coherent thought he could manage before once again falling into blackness.

"Whoa!" Casey said forcefully as the man lost consciousness again and leaned heavily against her. They were only a couple of feet from the couch, but there was no way she could maneuver him that far now that he wasn't helping. He was just too heavy for her to manage. She awkwardly eased him to the floor as gently as she could and after a few minutes had him lying on his back only a few feet from the fireplace.

"Chloe, honey, I'm going to spend some time cleaning up his wounds and checking out his injuries. Do you think you could build us a fire? We don't want him to get too chilly."

"Okay, Aunt Casey." The child looked him over from head to toe. "He really is big. Are you sure he isn't going to hurt us?"

Casey raised an eyebrow. She doubted the man would be a physical threat to anybody for quite a while, but the fact that he was an FBI agent was definitely disturbing. She sighed. It was more than disturbing. It was downright dangerous. Still, she couldn't leave him out in the woods to die. Bringing him here had been her only option. Yet she knew the man's presence signaled that her time left in the cabin was limited and she would soon have to find a new place to live. She didn't want Chloe to worry about it, though. The child had been through enough.

"He's probably a very nice man, honey, but we won't know for sure until he wakes up. For now let's just be very careful about what we say around him, like I said before. He can't know who we are or why we're living here. Do you understand? No last names, no information about where we came from and no telling him about anything that happened in Florida, okay?"

"Okay." The child's lip quivered and Casey pulled her close and gave her a hug. "I know this isn't what we planned to do when we came up here, sweet pea, but life is precious. We can't leave this man out in the woods to die because of our secrets. God wants us to always love our neighbors and help other people whenever we can, not just when it's convenient."

"But what if he's mean? What if he tries to hurt us?"

Casey grimaced as Chloe's words tore at her heart. No ten-year-old girl should have to live in fear, but her young niece had already lived a lifetime's worth of trepidation. "He's injured really badly, Chloe. He's not going to be doing anything to anybody for a while. But once he starts getting better, if he tries to hurt you in any way, all you have to do is scream and I'll come running to stop him. I'll protect you. I promise." She flicked the girl's nose playfully. "Now run and get my doctor bag for me while I get some things I need out of the kitchen."

The girl darted away and Casey watched her go, then turned back to her patient. She hoped she had enough of the correct supplies to do what she needed to help this man under these primitive conditions. At least she had confidence in her training. She had completed four years of medical school and had been on her way to a residency program in the Atlanta area only five short months ago, but that life seemed like almost a dream at this point. Since then, her entire world had been upended. She had given up her future and everything else in her life all to make sure Chloe would be safe. The sacrifice had been worth it, and she would do it again in a heartbeat, but she couldn't deny it felt good to be practicing medicine again. She'd loved learning to be a doctor and finding ways to help people get better. It had always been her dream, ever since she was a child.

She covered the man with a green cotton quilt, then went into the kitchen, got a large bowl of water and started heating it in the microwave. Then she grabbed a pair of scissors and a few other items she needed from the drawers. When the water was warm, she took it back into the living room beside the man, then took the scissors and cut away enough of his clothing to expose and treat the wounds. Chloe had brought her medical bag and also gotten a small fire going, then disappeared. Casey knew the child had probably gone back into the bedroom with a book and was silently glad that Chloe hadn't wanted to watch her work. Cleaning and treating this man's injuries wasn't going to be pretty.

She opened her medical bag and was instantly thankful that she always kept it stocked in case of an emergency. She had never expected an emergency of this proportion, however, and she rummaged through the bag's contents, hoping she would find sufficient supplies for closing his wounds. The bleeding had stopped on his leg and shoulder, so she focused on the wound on his side that was definitely the most life threatening. She checked for internal bleeding and said a silent prayer, hoping that the bullet hadn't hit any vital organs. Seeing none of the telltale signs, she cleaned the damaged area and started carefully stitching the skin together, thankful that the man was unconscious and unable to feel the pain that would undoubtedly haunt him when he woke up again.

After she had finished treating that injury, Casey turned her focus to the gash in the man's forehead. It was a deep slash and it took her quite a while to complete her work. She had not trained to be a plastic surgeon—or even a general surgeon—but she tried her best to keep her stitches small and even to minimize the scar. The man had dark brown hair in a very short, clean-cut style, but if he grew it out a tad on top, he could probably cover the scar with very little effort.

When she finished, she sat back and rested for a minute, taking stock of her handiwork. So far, so good. She looked carefully at the man's face. He was actually kind of handsome, in a military sort of way. He had strong features, including deep-set eyes, high, chiseled cheekbones and a wide, authoritative jaw.

Again she wondered what had brought him out here to the mountains. She'd only been living here about five months and didn't know any of her neighbors, but she still couldn't imagine why an FBI agent would be in this neck of the woods. Who had those other men been? Criminals he'd been trying to arrest? She blew out a breath and reminded herself to stay focused on her task. Wondering wouldn't bring her any answers right now.

She continued her work. At some point he would probably answer all of her questions if she could just get him healthy again.

The leg wound was next. The man moved a little as she worked but then seemed to lose consciousness once again. Casey said another silent prayer of thankfulness, glad that he was again out cold so he didn't feel the pain. All she had with her was a local anesthetic, and it wouldn't do much to help the throbbing he would have been feeling if he'd been conscious. She was especially not looking forward to digging the bullet out of his shoulder without the proper analgesic, but after completing her stitching on the leg wound, she took a fortifying breath and started her work.

About an hour later, with sweat covering her brow, she'd finished the last of her surgeries and had dressed all of his wounds. She pulled off the rubber gloves she had been wearing and tossed them into the bowl of bloody towels, then checked his pulse and breathing one more time. Everything looked good and his pulse was strong. What he needed now was rest and time to heal. She covered him with a blanket again and leaned back, exhausted.

She paused a moment, then reached for the wallet that she had removed from his pocket. He had a law enforcement shield on one side, and on the other a couple of credit cards and his driver's license. There was some cash inside, but she didn't bother counting it—it was none of her business. But she refused to feel guilty for flipping out the license and examining the picture and the other information. She had a right to know the name of the man she'd let into her home.

The driver's license definitely showed the man lying before her. According to the small print, his name was Jack Mitchell and he hailed from Charlotte, North Carolina. She closed her eyes and said a prayer for Jack Mitchell. Whether he survived or not was in God's hands now. She could do nothing else for him but pray.

# THREE

Casey adjusted the volume on the TV set, then sat back. The newswoman was interviewing a large Latino man who was identified as FBI unit chief José Mendoza. He was grim and stone faced and his expression was haggard, as if he didn't want to accept what was unfolding around him. Crime-scene tape fluttered behind them and red-and-blue police lights lit up the scene and cast shadows around the apartment building's parking lot.

A blue sedan was parked in the background and a group of men and women wearing FBI jackets surrounded the open trunk. Casey could just make out a thick piece of plastic hanging over the edge that seemed smudged with blood. Her heartbeat increased. That car had to be the one she'd seen racing away from the mountain after Jack Mitchell had been shot. The man in the trunk had to be the other victim the men had loaded inside. She leaned forward, eager to find out more about what was going on.

"Chief Mendoza, I understand that the victim's name is Milo Denton. Can you tell us anything about him?"

Mendoza shrugged. "I can tell you he was a private investigator from Raleigh. We've already notified his family."

"Was he shot?"

"Yes ma'am, the victim did sustain a bullet wound. We'll know more after the local medical examiner has a chance to process the scene and complete her investigation."

"Did anyone hear the gunshots?"

The chief shook his head. "No one has come forward so far. We're asking anyone with information about this situation to call our FBI hotline." The number ran along the bottom of the television screen.

"Do you know if he was killed in that car or at another location?" the newswoman pressed, motioning toward the blue sedan.

Casey noticed a look of discomfort cross the man's face. "We're not sure yet. It's too early and I'd only be speculating at this point. You'll have to give us a chance to do our job and perform a thorough investigation. Once we're finished, we'll issue a full report."

"Of course. Can you tell us who that car belongs to?"

"No comment. Now, if you don't mind…" He turned to head to the crime scene, but the newswoman followed him.

"Can you tell us how the body was discovered?"

"Anonymous tip."

"And why is the FBI involved? Have you been called in to aid the local police with the investigation?"

Mendoza grimaced. "I'm afraid that's all I can say right now. I need to get back to work."

The newswoman raised an eyebrow but turned back to the camera. "Well, ladies and gentleman, to recap, the body of private investigator Milo Denton was just discovered in the trunk of a car at the Midtown Apartment complex. Apparently Mr. Denton was the victim of gun violence, and both the FBI and local police are investigating at the scene. Be sure to tune in at six for a complete update."

Casey turned the TV off, disturbed by what she'd heard and more confused than ever. It seemed like the shooters had wanted the body to be discovered. Only they could have known to call in the "anonymous tip." Who was this Milo Denton, and how did he fit into the puzzle? And why had he been shooting at Jack yesterday?

She turned and dabbed Jack's lips with the washcloth. There was no use speculating. Answers would come eventually. She rewet the cloth and touched his lips again, wishing she had a proper IV setup so she could give the man the fluids he needed. He was still unconscious, but he didn't have a fever so far and she knew that she should count her blessings. She reached for her medical bag and began changing his bandages, carefully examining each wound for signs of infection. He was exactly where she expected him to be with his recovery, but she couldn't stop herself from worrying. What if he died? What would she do with him then?

"Jaime? Jaime, is that you?"

Casey startled at his words. His voice was a mere whisper, but he was waking up and obviously disoriented. "Jaime, it hurts."

She gently took his hand and ran her fingers over the skin in a soothing motion then squeezed lightly. "Shh. Don't worry. You're going to be okay. Just try to rest."

He seemed placated by her words and drifted

off again and she wondered for a moment who Jaime was. It was apparently someone important to him. A girlfriend…or a wife? He wasn't wearing a wedding ring, but she'd heard that some law enforcement agents didn't when they were on duty.

She finished changing the rest of the bandages, then gathered the old ones and leaned back. She was worried about him dying, but she almost had bigger problems if he lived. He was an FBI agent, and FBI agents were experts at discovering the truth. They were trained investigators, and the last thing she needed was someone asking questions about her and Chloe. Still, she couldn't regret her decision to help him. He definitely would have died if she'd left him in the forest. Somehow she and Chloe would make it through this latest challenge. All she had to do now was figure out how.

A few days later Jack opened his eyes and groaned. Every muscle in his body seemed to hurt, and pain radiated from each of his wounds. He suddenly became aware of a girl about ten years old leaning over him and touching his lips with a wet cloth. He swallowed hard, his mouth incredibly dry.

"Water...please."

The girl's eyes widened when she realized he was conscious. "Aunt Casey! He's awake! He just said something. Come here, come here!"

A few seconds later the woman he had mistaken for a princess stood before him with a grin on her face. "Hello, Agent Mitchell. Welcome back to the living." She felt his forehead. "Not a bit of fever. You are definitely on the mend."

The girl smiled at her aunt. "You did it, Aunt Casey! He's alive!"

"God did it," the lady corrected gently. "I just helped out a little."

Jack was happy to be breathing, but his immediate need was for something to drink. He felt as if he'd swallowed a cup full of sand. "Water..."

"Of course," Casey answered. "Let's get you up a little bit first. Chloe, you put the straw up to his mouth once I lean him forward so he won't choke." She put her arms behind his back and gently lifted him forward, being careful to stay away from his shoulder wound. It hurt to move, but it felt so good to take a drink from the straw that he ignored the pain. He finished and Casey let him gently lie back down on the floor.

He looked around the small room and took in his surroundings. There was a small fire in the grate, and the rest of the room was obviously a log cabin with rustic yet comfortable furnishings. His eyes returned to the two ladies that were watching him closely. "Where am I?"

"You're sharing our cabin," the lady answered. "My name is Casey, and this is my niece, Chloe." She paused. "I found you in the woods. You had been shot, so I brought you here to try to help you."

Jack soaked in the information and searched for the memories. Bits and pieces of information flitted around in his brain. The last thing he clearly remembered was Stevens aiming his weapon at him and the bullet knocking him to the ground, and then a princess hovering over him. He looked back at Casey. She was definitely his princess. He remembered the clear blue eyes, but little else about how he had ended up on the floor in this cabin.

He looked around again, considering the bucolic setting. All in all, it was probably a good thing that she had brought him here. His life was obviously in danger, and Stevens could have very well finished him off for good if he had shown up in a public place in his current condition. He was clearly unable to defend himself. Still, he wondered why the woman hadn't taken him to a hospital like most people would have done. He turned back to Casey and decided it was time to get some answers.

"Why not a hospital?"

The woman's blue eyes quickly darted away for a moment, and Jack instantly knew that something wasn't quite right.

"The nearest hospital is quite a distance away and I wasn't sure you'd make it. You had lost a lot of blood."

Jack mulled over her answer. He didn't think she was lying, but she was definitely hiding something. His brain seemed foggy and he felt very weak and disoriented, but his investigator instincts told him that there was more to the story than she was telling him.

"How long have I been here?"

"Four days. You've been drifting in and out of consciousness, which is to be expected."

He looked around at his makeshift bed. They had given him a pillow and blankets, and he was lying on a green braided carpet. "Why am I on the floor?" he asked.

"Because you weigh a ton!" Chloe blurted, then shyly shrank back. The two women shared a laugh, and Casey tugged on Chloe's braid affectionately and received a smile for her efforts.

Casey's expression seemed somewhat relieved that the conversation had shifted and Jack noticed that her posture seemed tense. Yes, something definitely wasn't right here, but he didn't get the sense that he was in any danger with them. On the contrary, they had saved his life.

"We tried to get you to the couch, but you passed out and we just couldn't manage to get you up there," Casey said. "You're a pretty big guy, Agent Mitchell. You're lucky we got you in as far as we did."

"Jack," he corrected. "Please. Call me Jack."

"Well, Jack, now that you're awake, do you want us to help you up to the couch? It might be more comfortable."

"No, not right now. I'm okay right here." Just that small bit of conversation had tired him out and he felt himself becoming drowsy.

Casey noticed and felt his forehead again, then picked up the cup he had used and leaned back. "Okay. Chloe, let's let our friend get some more rest. Can you throw another log on the fire? I'm going to go back outside and chop the rest of that wood."

Jack felt a little strange to be lying on a floor out of commission while a woman was outside chopping wood, but there wasn't much he could do about it. This whole scenario seemed strange and out of place, and he couldn't seem to make sense of any of it. A host of questions floated around in his mind, but for now, he let sleep consume him.

The next time he awoke Casey was sitting by his side and gently changing his bandages. It was obviously later in the day and the evening sunlight was barely coming through the windows. The pain was a little less severe, but still throbbed at even the smallest movement. At least his head seemed clear and he was able to think straight for a change.

"Aspirin. Do you have any aspirin?"

Casey nodded. "Sure thing, Agent Mitchell... ah, Jack." She reached for a bottle that was on the end table, took out two tablets and helped him hold his head up enough to take them with water from a straw. "They're actually a little stronger than aspirin and might make you a little drowsy." Jack raised an eyebrow but didn't question her about the pills. He had so many questions at this point that what type of pain medicine she was giving him was pretty far down the list.

"So you're the one who stitched me up, right?"

"That's right."

"What was the damage?"

"You got shot four times. Your leg injury missed the bone and is just a flesh wound. With some physical therapy you should heal up quite nicely. The gash on your forehead is the same. There was a lot of blood, but no bone damage. The one on the side there is a testament to God's grace—it just missed your vital organs by a hair. Your shoulder wound also missed the bone, but I had to dig out the bullet." She held up a little bag that was sitting on the end table. "I saved it for you as a souvenir." She gave him a soft smile. "All in all, it's amazing that you weren't hurt any worse. I was really worried that you'd go into shock because of all of the blood loss or that you'd have internal bleeding, but you've pulled through amazingly well."

He wrinkled his brow. "Are you a doctor?"

Casey shook her head. "No, but I've had some medical training."

"Enough to operate on my shoulder and take out the bullet?"

"Apparently." She put the bag back on the table and moved as if she were going to get up, but he grabbed her arm and stopped her escape. Her expression was guarded.

"Do you have my gun?"

"I do, but I unloaded it and put it away. I didn't want Chloe to get curious."

He loosened his grip. That made sense. Children and guns didn't mix. "What about my satchel? It was black leather with a silver buckle. Do you have it?" He tried to remember what had happened to it. Had Stevens taken it? A foggy memory seemed to suggest that, but he couldn't be sure. All he could really remember was the fire in Stevens's eyes right before he had pulled the trigger.

Casey shook her head again. "No. I didn't see a satchel anywhere around when I found you."

That was disappointing. No, it was devastating. The laptop and papers he'd discovered were the only lead he'd found. He'd been desperately hoping that they held evidence that would actually support his theories. Now he was virtually back to square one in his investigation. No, worse than square one, because this time he didn't even have a partner to watch his back—or shove a knife in it.

He grimaced as he remembered Stevens's betrayal. His partner's reprehensible acts caused a wave of anger to surge within him, and he fisted his hands and tried to sit up. Casey reached over and gently pushed him back down. "I don't think moving around right now is a really great idea."

"I need to get that bag," he said roughly.

Casey nodded. "Okay. I can go look for it later, but right now you need to rest. You can't go gallivanting around the countryside until you've healed up. If it's still there now, it will still be there in an hour or so. Right? I promise I'll go look for it when I go out in a few minutes."

Jack groaned as pain shot through his wounds, and he quit moving. He closed his eyes for a moment while he regrouped, then opened them again and glanced at the way he was dressed. "Where did these clothes come from?" He was clad in gray shorts and a navy T-shirt—neither of which he recognized.

"This cabin belongs to a friend of mine, and you two are about the same size. He had some spare clothes in a drawer, so I borrowed them for you. I know he won't mind."

Jack took the information in. He knew he was asking a lot of questions all at once, but he just couldn't help himself. "You said I've been here four days, right?"

"Yes," she agreed.

"Four days, and you still didn't want to call an

ambulance?" He paused, but didn't get a reply. "Does anyone else know I'm here?"

Jack could see the hesitance in her eyes. When she answered, her voice was shaking. "No. We don't have a phone and we live in a very remote area."

He raised an eyebrow at her and she rushed on with her explanation. "Don't get the wrong idea. You're not a prisoner. Whenever you're ready, I'll drive you down the mountain and take you to a hospital or wherever you want to go."

He reached over and grabbed her arm. "What if I said I was ready now?" He wasn't really. He still needed to discover the extent of his partner's betrayal and talk to his unit chief before he showed his face in public. Jack also knew he was in no condition to travel anywhere, yet he wanted to know her response just the same.

She looked a bit surprised but finally shrugged. "Then I'll drive you down. Just let me get my coat."

A moment passed, then another as he gauged her reaction. Finally he sank back. "I doubt I could make it to the car yet. I'd better stay a couple more days." He squeezed her arm, then released her. Although he knew something wasn't right about her situation, he was pretty sure she meant him no harm. In fact, it was obvious that he would have died if she hadn't come to his aid. She was definitely hiding something, but whatever her secret was, she'd risked it by taking him in, with nothing to gain from helping him.

"Thank you, Princess, for everything you've done. You saved my life."

She looked at him and their eyes met. "You're welcome."

He had never seen such striking eyes outside of a storybook. They were such a clear blue that he felt like he was looking at a warm summer sky. She had her hair pulled back in a ponytail again, which only served to accent her high cheekbones and full lips. He guessed that she was in her late twenties, which seemed odd to him because most women in their twenties that he knew didn't live out in the middle of nowhere with a young girl. What was she doing out here? And where were Chloe's parents?

"How long have you been living here?" he asked, and was immediately alerted when her eyes darted away again.

She seemed to be considering something, because eventually she made a decision and looked back at him with determination written all over her face.

"Look, Jack, I might as well tell you up-front. We value our privacy out here. You're welcome to stay as long as you need to recuperate, but please don't ask a lot of questions. I won't lie to you, but I won't answer you, either. Okay?"

Jack studied her carefully. He didn't believe for one minute that her reticence was due to privacy concerns, but he could be patient if he needed to. If he paid close attention, both Casey and Chloe would probably let bits of information slip in normal conversation. Being an investigator was too ingrained in him to just let this mystery go. And that meant he had to try to ask at least one more question.

"Can you at least tell me your name?"

She looked surprised. "I already told you. It's Casey."

"Casey what?"

"Just Casey is fine."

Jack leaned toward her, then grimaced as pain shot through his shoulder. "Look, I'm not trying to give you a hard time or be rude, but you must realize that I'm an FBI agent, and your behavior is suspicious, even for a woman who values her privacy."

"I can't help that, Jack. I'm not a princess and I'm not a puzzle. I'm just a woman who enjoys a quiet life who's trying to make her way through the world." She gave him a smile that told him the subject was closed, then picked up the old bandages and disappeared. He watched her go, more intrigued than ever.

What was her story? Better yet, what was her full name? And most importantly, what had happened that made her feel she had to hide? She was brave enough to rescue a stranger and perform surgeries to save his life. So why did she seem so afraid?

# FOUR

Jack shifted on the couch, still unable to find a comfortable way to lie that didn't aggravate his wounds. He reached for the remote, hoping for a distraction, and started flipping through the channels. There wasn't much on, but the midday news was just starting. He rolled his eyes at a story about a local politician and was about to change the channel when the image switched to a reporter standing in front of his apartment complex.

"Five days ago, the body of private investigator Milo Denton was found in the trunk of a car in this parking lot at the Midtown Apartments. Mr. Denton died from a gunshot wound, and was a person of interest in an FBI conspiracy investigation. Channel Five news has just learned that the car in question belongs to FBI agent Jack Mitchell. Agent Mitchell was reported missing the same day that Mr. Denton's body was discovered. Foul play is suspected. Anyone with news of Agent Mitchell's whereabouts is requested to call the FBI hotline at the number on the bottom of your screen."

A photo of Jack flashed across the screen along with a toll-free number and texting instructions.

Jack grimaced and he looked quickly for any sign of Casey or Chloe. Neither was in hearing distance of the TV. He turned the set off and put the remote back on the end table, hoping they hadn't heard the news story. The last thing he wanted was to drag them into the middle of his mess and make them afraid of him. Casey was probably already wondering why he had been shot and left for dead out in the woods, but so far she hadn't asked, and he hadn't volunteered the information.

What he needed was to get to a phone and call his unit chief to explain what happened and get Stevens and his cohort apprehended, but the task seemed impossible in his current situation. Casey had already said that she didn't have a phone, and he was still in no condition to walk—so getting in a car and driving down the mountain was out of the question.

Even if he had a way to make contact, though,

he wasn't sure that was the best course of action yet. By now, Stevens had to know that Jack wasn't dead. His partner would be looking for him to finish off the job—that much was certain. And from the looks of the news report, he'd already started blackening Jack's reputation. If Jack went somewhere public, he'd run the risk of being turned in by anyone who had seen the news story. And once he was in custody, he'd be at his ex-partner's mercy.

Even telephoning wasn't safe. Phone calls could be traced, and Stevens had already tried to kill him once. He didn't want to give the man a second chance until he was strong enough to defend himself.

For almost a year the two of them had been working on a conspiracy case that included some very powerful players. Jack believed that the head of the scheme was a district attorney named Matt Colby. The evidence seemed to indicate that Colby was fixing cases for profit at the federal courthouse in Raleigh. According to his theory, the D.A. would hire someone to destroy the evidence or somehow orchestrate "reasonable doubt" and then dismiss the charges so the defendant would go free. Afterward, the D.A. would collect a hefty fee from the defendant.

Jack hadn't been able to prove his theory yet because so far the evidence had all been circumstantial, but his unit chief, José Mendoza, had given him lots of room in the investigation. If the D.A. was dirty, it was their job to clean up the mess, and Mendoza was as determined as Jack to stop the buying and selling of justice. It was just plain wrong.

Jack had followed the clues and found a link that suggested the D.A. was hiring Milo Denton to fix the cases. When he'd found out Denton owned a cabin up near the national forest, which he used sometimes on the weekends, he'd secured a warrant and come up to check it out. He'd had no reason to question his partner's story when Stevens claimed he was chasing another lead and couldn't join Jack on the search.

The place had been empty when he'd arrived and after forcing the door, he'd found some bank statements, a notebook filled with handwritten notes and a laptop computer that he'd hoped would have broken the case wide open. Now all of that evidence had disappeared. Casey had returned to the woods to look for it, but had reported that the satchel was nowhere to be found. Stevens had definitely taken it with him, and probably destroyed all of the evidence or altered it to make Jack look guilty and throw suspicion off himself.

He balled his hands into fists as the frustration ate away at him. His car had obviously been discovered, but he doubted his tablet was anywhere to be found. Jack had carried the iPad with him everywhere and had meticulous notes inside about his investigations. Jack was a technology fan and had loved the tablet from day one since it let him write notes, read documents and do lightning-fast research whenever he needed to.

Jack was confident that Stevens couldn't have read Jack's encrypted files if the computer had ended up in his hands, but he could hide or destroy the tablet and all the information it held. And once that data was lost, Jack doubted he could recover it—he had been terrible about backing up his notes.

He laughed bitterly to himself. Even if his notes were recovered, nothing in them would incriminate Stevens. He had been truly surprised to see his partner pull a gun on him in the woods, and the betrayal still ate away at him. Still, losing the notes would be a huge setback and would hinder any other law enforcement personnel that tried to continue the investigation. Without Denton's computer or papers and Jack's iPad, the case against Colby and his cohorts was at a complete standstill. And with Stevens putting Denton's body in Jack's trunk and throwing suspicion on him, the investigation had taken a dangerous and unsuspected turn.

If Stevens discovered his whereabouts and eliminated him, then it wouldn't take much to create some fake evidence that incriminated Jack for the entire conspiracy. Stevens, the D.A. and the others would continue to get away with their schemes and perversion of justice. Jack couldn't let that happen.

He was not a patient man, but for now he would have to rest and heal until he was strong enough to defend himself and make sure the guilty parties paid for their crimes.

Casey flipped the page on the *Reader's Digest* magazine, enjoying the fire. She glanced over at Jack, who was dozing lightly on the couch. She rarely read magazines, but found that she needed a diversion from the worry that was eating away at her. It had been a week since the shooting, and Jack was slowly recovering. He had backed off a little with his questions, but she knew that he was paying careful attention to what she and Chloe said and did whenever they were together.

She didn't regret saving Jack's life, but why, oh, why did he have to be a law enforcement officer? That fact alone put her entire existence in jeopardy.

She flipped another page and read the "Humor in Uniform" section, laughed softly at a couple of the stories, then flipped again. The next section was some story about a police drama, but it held no appeal for her. She couldn't see the police as heroes—not after all the times police friends of her brother-in-law had ignored the danger Chloe and her mother were in.

Her sister's murder was still fresh in Casey's mind, and also the way that law enforcement had botched the case. The investigation had been a joke since they'd started, and of course when push came to shove, they hadn't found enough evidence to prosecute the murderer. Now he was out free, gloating in his successful thwarting of the law. It was a bitter pill to swallow.

Casey didn't enjoy hiding out in the woods, but she didn't have much choice. Her sister had been murdered by her husband, Chloe's father, and if Casey hadn't taken Chloe and disappeared with her, Casey was convinced that the little girl would have also become a victim to the monster her sister had married.

Even though she knew she'd done the right thing, Casey was wanted by the police and would be arrested for kidnapping if anyone discovered her whereabouts. Even worse, though, was the fact that if they were found, Chloe would be returned to her father's custody. Casey had to make sure that didn't happen—no matter what the cost.

She glanced over at Jack. He looked dangerous himself right now, in spite of his wounds. He hadn't shaved since he'd arrived and the shadow of his beard gave him a menacing appearance. Her heart squeezed in her chest. He was a lawman. He could arrest her if he found out who she was and what she'd done. Why hadn't she taken him to a hospital after he'd regained consciousness? Had she made a huge mistake?

She sighed. She already knew the answer to her question. He was obviously in danger and needed her help. If the men who had tried to kill him hadn't stopped in the forest, why would they hesitate to kill him lying in a hospital bed when he was at his most vulnerable? She just had to hope and pray that he would never discover her secrets.

She put the magazine away and reached for the remote, making sure the volume was turned down low on the TV as she turned it on. An *I*

*Love Lucy* rerun was on, but she changed the channel and passed by two shopping channels before she ended up on a news program. She almost changed the channel again, but Jack's picture up in the right-hand corner of the screen caught her attention.

"Jack? Jack, you're on TV." She got up and nudged him, then turned up the volume and moved the screen so he could see it, as well. He blinked a couple of times as he woke up, but quickly focused on the anchorwoman's words.

"...Jack Mitchell, a special agent with the FBI from the Charlotte office, is still missing. He was last seen on November 5 in the vicinity of Stanfield, and is wanted for questioning in connection to the murder of a local private investigator, Milo Denton. Mr. Denton's body was recovered in the trunk of Agent Mitchell's car. Those with information about Agent Mitchell's whereabouts are encouraged to call the FBI tip line at 1-800-555-4532. In other news..."

Jack pulled himself to a sitting position and stared at the television, lost in thought, even though the story about him was over. Casey saw the frustration written on his face and wished she could do something to fix his situation. It couldn't be easy for him to have had someone shoot him and leave him for dead. And now they were suggesting he was guilty of murder! What she'd seen hadn't been murder. It had been a law enforcement officer defending himself from an ambush. She didn't know all of the details surrounding the shooting, but her intuition told her that Jack was the victim, not a criminal.

She sighed. She couldn't fix his problems with the authorities, but at least she could help him get healthy again.

"Are you hungry? I've got some chicken soup I can heat up."

"Don't call that number. Please, Casey."

"I won't. I don't have a phone, remember?"

"I know, but you have to go out now and then to restock your supplies. You'll have access to a phone, and you'll probably be tempted."

"I won't call, Jack. I promise."

She looked him in the eye, hoping he could see her sincerity. He was watching her so closely she felt like a specimen under a microscope. It was painfully obvious that despite his own problems, he was frightfully acute, and was studying her, looking for answers. His scrutiny made her nervous and she took a step back, then nervously hid her hands when she realized they were trembling. He continued to gaze at her despite her retreat, but finally, he nodded. "Sure. Soup sounds good."

Casey escaped to the kitchen and leaned heavily against the counter as worry consumed her. His perusal had shaken her so badly that her stomach had twisted into knots. He was a trained investigator. He probably saw more in his injured state than most people saw after a week of being near someone.

She felt intimidated and at the same time filled with fear. Even if she drove him back to town tomorrow, would he let his suspicions die and leave them alone? She laughed to herself. Probably not. Although a part of her remained hopeful, the more practical side knew she would have to find a new place to live with Chloe as soon as Jack healed and returned to his world. She just couldn't risk him coming back and arresting her.

She started preparing the soup as she mulled over the possibilities. This cabin was owned by the family of one of her classmates. She didn't know anybody else that had something similar where they could hide. She had a small amount of money with them, but if she used it for rent, she wouldn't be able to stay hidden for very long. The problem was they'd had to leave Florida in such a hurry that she hadn't been able to perfect her plans and prepare for every contingency; now that lack of planning was coming back to bite her.

The soup started simmering, and she poured it into a bowl and carried it back out to her guest.

"Here you go. Nice and hot." She set down the food and then propped Jack up with pillows so he could manage to drink the broth without choking. Once she had him at the proper angle, she started spooning him the soup, blowing on it gently before raising the spoon to his lips.

He watched her intently with his dark brown eyes and she felt a strange warmth come over her and a tingling sensation shoot down her arms. A dribble of soup ran down his chin and she caught it with a cloth napkin. It was actually a very nice chin. She looked up and their eyes locked. Her mouth went dry and she couldn't think of a single thing to say.

He gave her a small smile. "I appreciate you taking such good care of me, Princess."

She looked down, but a moment later her eyes were pulled back to his like a magnet. He had very nice eyes, too, she realized with a jolt. Nice eyes and a very handsome face.

"I'm no princess."

"You are to me," he answered quietly.

She blushed. It had been a long time since anyone had paid her such a simple yet pleasing compliment. She suddenly wondered about his background and realized she knew very little about the man. Would he share information with her, even though she wasn't willing to do the same? She figured there was no harm in asking.

"So what brought you into my neck of the woods anyway? We get very few visitors out here."

Jack swallowed another spoonful of broth. Now that she had seen the news story, he must have realized that there was no sense keeping it a secret, because a moment later, he began to explain.

"About a month ago I discovered some irregularities with some cases I had worked. Evidence suddenly disappeared in one case, and in another the evidence was suspiciously destroyed, supposedly by accident. I started investigating, but kept hitting roadblocks that shouldn't have been there. Eventually things started coming together, and everything was pointing toward the district attorney, a man named Matt Colby. I think he's tampering with evidence so he can fix trials and earn a large profit on the side. They don't pay us civil servants very much."

He paused for a moment and shifted on the couch. "Recently, I found a connection between the D.A. and Milo Denton, a local private investigator. I think Denton was one of the people helping destroy evidence. It turns out Denton owned a cabin out here where he lived on occasion, so I came to check it out and see if there were any clues about the other conspirators. It was a long shot, but I had very few leads. I found a laptop and some documents in the cabin—I put them in that satchel I asked you to find. I'd hoped to have a chance to go through them once I got back to the office, but I never managed that. As soon as I left the cabin, I found myself in an ambush. I did shoot Denton, the man they found in my car, but you have to believe me, Casey—it was self-defense. And I didn't hide the body. The other men did that to try to cast suspicion on me."

"How did they know you were at the cabin in the first place?"

Jack let out a small, bitter laugh. "I told them. Or at least, I told my partner where I was planning to go. Little did I know that he was one of the accomplices. Apparently I was getting too close to the truth. He shot me and left me for dead."

Casey leaned back, shocked by the revelation.

"That was your partner? He was the one that did this?" Her muscles tensed. "Will he be back?"

Jack nodded. "I would imagine so. Once they got Denton taken care of, I would imagine they came back looking for me. They're probably a little worried since they haven't found me. Who knows what story they're passing around down at the office? It's going to take some work to clear my name and prove my partner's involvement in all of this."

Casey mulled over his words. "I'm sorry I couldn't find that satchel you wanted. They must have taken it with them when they left."

Jack closed his eyes and fisted his hands, obviously angry and distressed. Finally he opened his eyes again and made a slight motion with his good right hand. "How much did you actually see when I got shot?"

Casey shrugged. She couldn't tell him the truth about that. If he knew she'd seen the whole thing, he'd want her to make an official statement. There was no way she could ever testify in court about what had happened. She chose to avoid the question. "I heard some shooting when I was out taking a run. I went down to investigate and found you bleeding on the ground."

Jack paused, considering her answer. It was

obvious that he'd noted her curt response and lack of detail. He tried again. "Did you get a good look at the shooters' faces?"

Casey tried to change the subject. "I think it's time to change your bandages. I'll go get the supplies."

Jack leaned back and watched her go. When she returned, there was a look of consternation on his face. "You sure are an enigma, Princess, and I just can't figure you out. Why so secretive?"

She didn't answer and focused on her work, starting to change his leg bandages first.

He watched in silence for a few moments, then pushed forward. "Look, I've considered the possibilities, and maybe my law enforcement background is clouding my thinking, but I can't think of a single positive reason for your hesitance." He paused and ran his good hand through his hair. "Are you hiding from someone?"

She didn't answer, so he tried again. "Are you in trouble with the law?"

She tensed at his question but finished with his leg and turned her attention to his side. This FBI agent was entirely too perceptive. She kept her eyes averted and focused on cutting the gauze for the bandage.

"Casey? I really need an answer. I promise I'll do whatever I can to help you. You saved my life. I won't forget that."

She didn't answer, and he gently grabbed her hand and stilled her work until she looked up at him.

"Casey? I know you don't know me from Adam, but please trust me. Let me repay the favor. Let me help you."

His fingers were warm and strong, and when she looked into his eyes, she could see his concern and caring. Still, the problems she faced were bigger than he could solve, even if he was an FBI agent. In fact, if he knew the truth, he'd have to arrest her right now and everything she had sacrificed would have been for naught.

"I can't, Jack. Please don't ask again. The less said the better."

He continued to hold her hand for a moment but finally released it, clearly disappointed. She changed the rest of his bandages in awkward silence, then took a deep breath and tried to brighten her countenance. "Would you like some more soup?"

He nodded and accepted the spoonful she offered, but his dark eyes seemed to be pulling her into their depths. Casey decided it was time to change the subject.

"Do you have a family?" she asked, breaking the silence. She actually really wanted to know the answer to that question. She knew she would be devastated if someone she loved was missing and she didn't know if they were alive or dead. It was the one thought that kept bothering her about keeping Jack's presence a secret. And who was that Jaime that he had called for?

Jack shook his head. "My parents were in a car crash a few years back, and I'm not married."

"No brothers or sisters?"

"One sister, six years younger. Ashley's a scientist, currently on a research trip down in South America. I'm glad she's not around to have to deal with all of this."

She offered him another spoonful. "Who is Jaime?"

His eyes widened and for a moment he just looked at her intently. "Wow. You surprised me with that one. How do you know about her?"

Casey shrugged. "I don't. You called out her name a couple of times when you were coming in and out of consciousness. I thought she must be important to you."

"She was my wife," he said quietly. "She died from cancer about a year ago."

Casey's eyes softened. "I'm so sorry, Jack. I didn't mean to bring up a sad memory."

"Actually, most of the memories are good ones. We didn't have a long time together, but what we had was special." He took a breath, apparently ready for a change in the topic. "How about yourself? Any family?"

Casey leaned back again, the soup bowl empty. "No. No one but Chloe."

"She seems like a sweet girl."

"She is," Casey agreed. "I'd do anything for her." She smiled to soften the tone of her voice. She was passionate about her niece and loved the little girl fiercely. She wasn't sure what the future held for either of them, but the man lying before her had already altered her circumstances in more ways than she could imagine. Only time would tell if her next home was somewhere safe or a jail cell.

"She calls you Aunt Casey," Jack said with a question in his voice.

"That's right. She's my niece."

"Where are her parents?"

Casey drew her lips together into a thin line.

Finally she spoke. "My sister was her mother, and she died almost six months ago."

"I'm sorry to hear that," Jack answered, his empathy genuine. "What about Chloe's father?"

Casey stood. "He's no longer an option." She smoothed his blanket, trying to hide how much his prying had affected her. Had she just given away too much information? It was time to escape. She hurriedly gathered up the old bandages and other supplies, then headed to the kitchen.

Jack watched Casey retreat, his mind full of questions. It sure sounded like Chloe had suffered through a traumatic year. Losing a mother would be hard on anyone. He leaned back and fisted his hands, running through other parts of the conversation, as well.

So he had called out for Jaime. Images of his wife filled his mind—Jaime smiling after eating a piece of fudge, Jaime laughing as the sun played in her hair, Jaime hooked to an IV in the hospital, a shadow of her former self. They had only been married for two short years before cancer stole her away from him. She had died only six months after they had learned of the diagnosis.

Had it really been a year since she had died?

He'd never thought he'd feel anything for a woman again after going through the pain of losing Jaime, but there was something about Casey that stirred him inside and made him feel things that he hadn't felt for a very long time. It was an odd sensation that he'd never expected, and didn't welcome, either. He wasn't ready to love again, and the thought of giving his heart away a second time seemed too risky to even consider.

He shook his head and tamped the feelings down deeply inside. This was ridiculous. He had only known Casey for a short stretch of time. Sure, Casey was attractive, but any emotions that he felt for her had to be based on gratitude because she had saved his life, nothing more.

And what was the secret she was hiding? It had to be something serious or she wouldn't be trying to bury it so desperately. Had she broken the law? Was she hiding from an old boyfriend or abusive husband? And how did Chloe fit into the mix? There were only so many reasons why Casey could be so secretive and hiding out in a mountain cabin. One way or another, he was determined to find out the truth. All he needed was a computer, access to the FBI databases and a few hours to discover her past. He was sure he could learn her story with just a few simple keystrokes.

But what would happen then? Would his discovery mean that he'd have to leave his safe haven…or maybe even arrest the woman who'd saved his life?

# FIVE

"Okay, Princess. I'm ready to walk."

Casey raised an eyebrow. "Oh, really?" Jack had slowly been sitting up more and more with each passing day, but walking more than a couple of feet hadn't been attempted as of yet. It had been a little over a week since he had been shot, though, and it made sense to give it a try. She set aside the novel she had been reading and came to his side to help him.

"How are you feeling?"

"A long way from my old self, but I've got to do this. I can't stay on your couch forever." He pushed himself up, grimacing as he put weight on his injured leg. Casey positioned herself under his arm and slowly they got him to a standing position.

"Where to?" she said, trying to distract him from the pain she knew he was feeling.

"The bathroom," he said, taking his first step.

It was slow going, but they eventually made it. She gave him some privacy once they arrived, but waited outside in the hallway in case he needed her help. A few minutes later he reappeared. His face was somewhat pale and his steps were short, but he was up and she could tell that he was pleased to finally be mobile again.

The happy mood was shattered when a knock on the front door startled them both.

Casey's eyes widened and she looked at Jack. "I never get visitors. Never. Stay here out of sight and let me see what's going on." She leaned him against the wall, then found Chloe doing schoolwork at the kitchen table and motioned for her to be quiet and stay put. Finally she headed to the entrance, just as the visitor started knocking again.

She couldn't see who was there through the front window, but she pushed aside the curtain anyway and could just barely make out the car parked in front of the cabin. It was a brown sedan and looked a lot like the one she'd seen the day of the shooting.

There was no peephole so she mustered her courage, then opened the door. There were two men standing there, both with dark hair and both wearing boots with guns strapped to their hips. The taller one was wearing a suit jacket and a white open-collared shirt, while the other had on jeans and a flannel shirt and looked much rougher around the edges.

She instantly recognized them as the men from the shooting.

A bolt of fear swept through her but she tamped it down the best she could and tried to act nonchalant.

"Can I help you?"

"Yes ma'am," the man with the jacket said in a deep, overly friendly voice. "I'm Agent Stevens with the FBI and this is Bill Fletcher, a consultant with the agency." He showed her his badge and ID, then pocketed them. "I don't want to scare you, but we're looking for a suspect wanted for one of our current murder investigations who might be in the area. He's a tall man, about six-three, with dark hair and brown eyes. He's probably injured." He opened a folder he was carrying and showed her a picture. It was a younger Jack wearing a suit and tie. "It's pretty remote up here. Have you seen any strangers in the area?"

Casey swallowed. "No, no strangers." Jack wasn't technically a stranger, she thought to herself. She had known him for over a full week now, and even though she didn't know much about him, she had been nursing him the entire time and definitely didn't consider him a stranger. "You said he murdered someone? Was it someone that lived up here?"

"No ma'am. I'm sure all your neighbors are safe. The crime happened somewhere else but we think he might have fled up here." He handed her a flyer that had Jack's picture on it and some basic information about him, along with some key phone numbers. "If you see him, you give us a call, all right? He's armed and very dangerous."

Casey nodded nervously. There was no reason to explain that she didn't have a phone so she couldn't be calling anyone, whether she wanted to or not. At this point she just wanted these men off her porch and as far away from her and Chloe as possible. "I understand. Thanks for letting me know. I'll definitely keep an eye out." She turned to go but the man put his arm on her door frame and stopped her retreat. When she turned back, his eyes were intense and penetrating as if he could see right through her.

"Are you okay, ma'am? You seem a little on edge."

"You scare me," she said truthfully. "I don't get many visitors up here, and now I've got two men with guns on my front porch talking to me about a wanted man who is on the loose. This doesn't happen to me every day."

The man considered her words, then moved his arm. "We didn't mean to scare you, ma'am. We've just got a job to do, and we need to find this man as soon as possible." He nodded to her, then to the other man. "You have a good day now and try not to worry."

She gave him a weak smile, hoping that the relief that she was feeling at their departure wasn't painted on her face. "Thank you."

She went back into the cabin and closed and locked the door, then peeked through the curtain again and watched the men return to their car. The window was open and she could just make out their words.

"Well, that got us nowhere. How many more of these mountain cabins do we have to visit before we call the day a complete waste of time?" The man who had been introduced as Bill Fletcher motioned with his hands toward her cabin as he spoke, frustration clearly evident.

The FBI agent, Stevens, shook his head and pulled out his keys. "I wouldn't call this a waste of time. We might have just discovered our first clue."

"What do you mean?" Fletcher asked, unbuttoning the top button of his flannel.

"Something's not right about that woman up there. She was too nervous, too jittery. I think she knows something."

Fletcher shrugged. "I didn't see anything unusual. She's a hermit and we freaked her out. Doesn't sound too odd to me."

"Maybe. But maybe she knows something."

"Well, what do you want to do about it?"

Stevens pulled out his keys. "I don't have enough for a warrant, but my gut is telling me that she's the one we need to keep an eye on."

"Do we have time to just sit around and 'keep an eye' on things? The D.A.'s already nervous about all of this, Brett. If we don't take care of Jack fast, he might send someone after us to take us out of the mix. We don't have time to waste. If you've got a feeling about her, let's go back right now and lean on her."

Stevens shrugged. "You're right about Colby, and I agree that he's a powerful adversary, and he's not known for his patience. But if I rush things without a warrant, I run the risk of getting sloppy. If that happens, I'll have even more loose ends to tie up, and I don't want any mistakes."

"You mean like putting Denton's body in the

back of Jack's car? Yeah, that wasn't one of your smartest moves."

Stevens opened his car door. "Look, how was I supposed to know the chief was going to grab jurisdiction and bring in the FBI crew? I thought the local police department would have been the ones called out to handle the case. It should have been open and shut, with the evidence only pointing to Jack. You know as well as I do that the local pathologist is a joke who would never have picked up on the forensics that are giving the chief so much heartburn. But no, I just can't catch a break."

Fletcher opened his door, as well. "Yeah. Just your luck. The FBI pathologist is the best in the whole Southeast. Smooth move, Stevens. I don't know how you convinced me to get mixed up in this whole mess in the first place."

"I didn't see you complaining on our last payday. You're making a heap of money to do as you're told and keep your mouth shut." He got in the car and Casey strained to hear the rest of the conversation. "Well, we've still got a lot of area we haven't even covered yet. Let's finish the first round, and if we don't find any other leads, we can come back and keep an eye on the house for a while. Maybe we'll see something that will help us figure out what's going on."

Fletcher shrugged as he got in, as well. "You're the boss. Let's grab something to eat, though, before we go any farther. I'm starving."

"You got it," Stevens agreed.

The car engine roared to life, and they turned it around and drove away.

Casey waited a moment, watching the plume of dirt follow their car down the long unpaved driveway to make sure they were really gone. Finally she remembered she had left Jack standing in the hall and rushed back to his side to aid him once again.

He was still propped where she had left him, but the effort to stay standing had taken a toll and a fine sheen of perspiration covered his brow. He was even paler now and she hurried to help him back to the couch.

"Who was it?" he asked weakly.

"Your friends from the forest—an Agent Stevens and another guy named Bill Fletcher. They're looking for you. I'm not sure they believed I didn't know where you are. In fact, I overheard one of them say they would come back if they didn't find any other leads."

Chloe was standing at the doorway to the

kitchen now, but she had heard their conversation and her eyes rounded in fear. "What are we going to do?"

"I'm not sure yet, but I'll come up with something," Casey said firmly. She helped get Jack settled, then went to her niece and enveloped her in a big hug. "Give me some time to think about this, sweetheart. Okay? Agent Mitchell and I will talk and we'll figure out something." She pulled back and playfully touched the girl's nose. "How's the math coming?"

Chloe made a face. "I'm really starting to hate word problems."

Casey squeezed her again, then took a step back and nudged her towards the table. "Don't give up. Just go step-by-step like we talked about. You'll figure them out." She motioned toward the couch. "Let Agent Mitchell and I talk for a bit, then we'll let you know our plans."

Chloe nodded, but there was still fear in her eyes and it broke Casey's heart to see it. The girl had already gone through so much. It wasn't fair that she was again in the middle of something very scary and very dangerous. Still, Casey couldn't regret helping Jack. She would never have forgiven herself if she had left him to die in the woods, and that was the only way she could have avoided this entire situation. Life was precious and valuable, and she was committed to saving a life whenever she was given the chance to do so.

She spent a few minutes getting Chloe started on her math, hoping that the distraction would keep her niece's mind off the men's visit. The girl struggled with the first few problems, but eventually seemed to put the fear aside and concentrate on the workbook. Finally Casey left her to finish the next two pages and went to join Jack on the couch.

When she spoke, her voice was shaking. "Okay, Jack. Tell me where we go from here. Those men gave me this flyer and said you're being investigated for murder, but that's just crazy. If you hadn't shot back, they would have killed you! The shots were coming from all over—you were just trying to defend yourself. You didn't have a choice!"

Jack raised an eyebrow. "So you saw that?"

Casey realized her mistake and twisted her hands. She moved as if to get off the couch, but he gently grabbed her arm and kept her from escaping. "You know, Casey, you can't always run away when the questions get hard. At some point you have to stand your ground." He took the flyer and studied it for a minute, then wadded it up and threw it into the fire. "As you said, it was absolutely self-defense, but they had to come up with some sort of story to explain the man's death and my disappearance. Apparently, blaming me for murder takes care of both of those problems, and also discredits me if I live long enough to tell what I know about them fixing cases."

He looked around the room and gritted his teeth as he considered his options. Right now his immediate concern was making sure Casey and Chloe were safe. He was so weak physically that he couldn't do much to protect them if—when—Stevens and Fletcher came back looking for him again, and that thought worried him above all else.

The two ladies would be in very serious danger if Stevens realized they had pulled him from the woods and saved his life, and Stevens would definitely kill them both if he knew that Casey had witnessed the shooting and could identify them in court.

He looked over at Casey and noted the worry on her face. How much of the shooting had she seen? What exactly did she know? He wanted to ask her some very specific questions, but he could tell that she was in no mood to answer him. He would just have to bide his time until the right opportunity arose.

"Can you bring me my gun?"

Casey raised an eyebrow but nodded, then left for a moment and returned with a plastic bag. He opened it and found his wallet, gun and cell phone. A separate bag contained a few loose bullets and the extra clip. He flipped open the cell phone and tried to turn it on, but the battery was dead. He doubted he would have had a signal out in this remote spot anyway.

True, Stevens has been able to receive a call at the shooting that had distracted him and probably saved Jack's life. But that had been a fluke. Cell service up in the mountains was spotty—Stevens had just happened to decide to kill Jack in a strong signal pocket. "Thanks for hanging on to all of this. Is it okay if I keep my weapon with me from now on? It might come in handy."

"I don't want a loaded gun around Chloe," Casey said firmly.

"How about I don't load it unless I need to? Would that be okay? You can explain to her that it's not a toy and she isn't to touch it."

Casey hesitated but finally nodded.

"Can you tell me what else the men at the door said to you?"

"They asked me if I had seen any strangers in the area." She shrugged. "Since I don't think you're very strange anymore, I said no."

Jack laughed as he reached for her hand and gave it a squeeze. Her skin was so soft and sweet that he didn't want to let go. The thought gave him pause. He wasn't looking for a relationship. Even if the timing hadn't been terrible with the murder charge hanging over his head, he didn't need the complication and especially didn't want to ever feel the pain of losing someone he cared about ever again. Still, he couldn't seem to keep away from Casey and felt compelled to touch her whenever she was within reach. What was wrong with him? He gently rubbed his thumb over the back of her hand, pleased that she didn't pull away, yet worried at the same time about the feelings stirring inside him that he couldn't seem to ignore.

"We need a plan for when they come back."

Casey's eyes widened. "You said when, not if. Are you sure they'll be back?"

"Yes. I guarantee it. They won't quit looking until they find me. Brett Stevens never did like loose ends. This one will haunt him until he knows I'm no longer a threat."

"What should we do?"

"Start packing."

# SIX

Three days later Jack was doing even better with the walking, even though he still felt weak and sore. Thankfully, Stevens and Fletcher hadn't returned, so they were able to stay put...for now. Casey wanted to hold off on leaving as long as possible, to give Jack a chance to heal without having to deal with traveling...and to give both of them a chance to come up with a new place to go that would keep them under the radar. They hadn't come up with one yet. The bags were packed and ready, though. They could leave at a moment's notice if they had to—which he suspected they would, soon.

He looked in the bathroom mirror and examined the sutures, gingerly touching the area near the wounds. They were healing up pretty well. Casey said she would probably remove the stitches later this afternoon or tomorrow. He looked even closer. Each stitch seemed to have been professionally done. The quality of Casey's medical care made him wonder even more about her past. She was definitely no novice. How did she possess such impressive medical skills? And why was someone with skills like that hiding out in this desolate place? It just didn't make sense.

His quest to find out more about Casey and Chloe had so far been a tremendous failure. Chloe had barely said ten words to him since he had arrived, and Casey did her best to avoid him unless she was tending to him. With very few exceptions, every time he had tried to start a conversation, she had shut him down with yes or no answers, and then disappeared. Occasionally she sat in the same room with him and read a book, but she always used the book as a barrier and wouldn't speak beyond what was necessary. She had nursed him with care and a soft touch, but so far she hadn't revealed anything more about her past. The less she talked, however, the more he felt driven to discover her secrets.

He was itching to get back to his computer and law enforcement databases so he could do some exploring. He knew there was a story here. Years of training and experience told him he probably wouldn't like the answers once he discovered them. Innocent people usually had nothing to hide, and Casey wouldn't even share her last name with him. But even though his instincts told him to be wary, he couldn't help feeling protective toward her. She had helped him, saved him, let him into her life and her home. Whatever her secrets were, she'd risked them to come to his aid. He wanted to repay the favor and help her with whatever it was that had her so scared.

He turned and limped slowly back into the living room area. Casey was outside somewhere, and Chloe was doing her schoolwork at the kitchen table, as she did most mornings. Casey was homeschooling the child and he had heard the two of them in the kitchen going over the latest lessons about an hour ago. He looked in and saw Chloe with her head back, staring at the ceiling.

"You doing okay in here?"

Chloe's head snapped forward at his words and she shrank down in her chair. "Yes. Fine."

Jack raised an eyebrow. The girl still seemed to be afraid of him, even after he'd been living at the cabin for almost two weeks. He pretty much had to move slowly because of his condition, but he still tried to limit his movements and appear as nonthreatening as possible whenever he was around her so he wouldn't frighten her even more. Was it normal for a child to be that skittish? He hadn't spent a lot of time around kids, but her behavior seemed odd even to him.

"What are you studying?"

"English," she said so softly that he had to strain to hear her.

"English? I did pretty well in English. Can I see what you're working on?"

Chloe seemed to consider his words, then finally nodded. Jack took a seat next to her and looked at the paper she handed him. It looked like she needed to write some sort of basic essay. He looked back at her and noticed that she had moved as far away from him as possible while still sitting on the chair. He wondered about her behavior. Had she been abused or attacked? Why was she so scared to be around him? The child was just as much of a puzzle as her aunt, and so far, he had learned very little about Chloe. It was time to give getting to know her a try.

"Have you picked a topic for your essay?"

Chloe shook her head. "No. That's where I'm stuck. It says I should pick something I really care about and write an essay describing it, but I don't know what to say."

Jack leaned back, hoping to give her the space

she needed to be comfortable. This was the first real conversation they'd had, and he didn't want to scare her off. "Well, have you ever had a pet, like a dog or a cat?"

Chloe shook her head again.

"Do you have a favorite toy?"

She gave this some thought, then finally nodded. "I used to have a stuffed bear that I really liked."

"Is it here at the cabin?"

"No, I had to leave it at my house when I left."

"You mean before you came to live here with your aunt Casey?"

"Yes. I don't know if it's still there or not."

"Why wouldn't it be?"

The girl pursed her lips together. "I don't know."

Jack ran his hands through his hair. "Where's your house, Chloe?"

The girl's eyes widened. "Aunt Casey said I'm not supposed to talk about that. She said everything that happened in Florida is a secret."

"Ah, okay," Jack responded, pleased that she hadn't realized that she had mentioned Florida. "Do you miss your home?"

The girl's face changed and she looked like

she was about to cry. "No. I don't ever want to go back."

Jack was startled by the information and wanted to ask for more explanation, but decided it was time to change the subject. He didn't want to upset the girl, or make Casey angry if Chloe mentioned the conversation later. If he could befriend the Chloe, maybe she would reveal more to him as their relationship developed. "Well, your assignment here says you need to write a topic sentence that tells what your essay is about, so how about you write a sentence about that bear you liked? Then it says you need to write a few descriptive sentences about the bear. You could answer questions like, does it have a name, is it a girl or a boy, what color is it, what kind of fur does it have, what games did you like to play together—things like that." He smiled at her. "What do you think? Will that help you get started?"

She smiled back at him and relaxed her stance a measure. "Yeah, I could do that."

"Great. Why don't you give it a try, and then let me see what you've written in a few minutes. Sound good? If you get stuck, we'll talk some more."

"Sure, Agent Mitchell."

"My name is Jack, Chloe. You can call me Jack."

He reached to pat her head in a friendly gesture, but she ducked to avoid his touch. He pulled back. This child had been hurt and hurt badly, that much was obvious. If he had to guess, he would also say that it was a man that had done the damage. It was abundantly clear that she was frightened of him. If a man had harmed her in some way, it would surely explain the child's jittery behavior.

"Well, I'm going back to the couch and I'll let you get at it. Okay?"

She nodded at him again with a look of relief on her face. He pulled himself up and headed back to the living room and the couch that had become his bed. He was getting a touch of cabin fever and had decided that once Casey returned, it was time to ask her to take him down the mountain. Hopefully she'd agree that he was up for a short ride. Although he was still weak, he needed to at least attempt to clear his name and stop Stevens and the D.A. before even more cases were thrown out and criminals were released. He worked the fingers on his left hand that was still in a sling and felt the burn as his muscles pulled. He knew his body still needed quite a bit more time to heal, but sometimes what he needed and what he actually got were two entirely different things.

Suddenly the front door swung open and Casey ran in, breathing hard. "The same car from before is coming up the road. It's them! And they're only about five minutes away. We have to get out of here!"

Jack didn't hesitate. He opened the drawer where they had stored his weapon and began loading the gun, then pocketed his ID, cell phone and the little bag that had the bullet Casey had dug out of his shoulder.

"Grab your bag," he said curtly. "I'll meet you at the car."

Casey nodded and hurried to the bedroom, then came back a few moments later carrying two suitcases and her medical bag slung over her shoulder. She dropped the luggage by the door, then grabbed a cloth tote from under the sink and threw in a jar of peanut butter and a few other items. "Let's go, Chloe. Grab your backpack and get in the car. Pronto."

Chloe stood frozen at the table, a look of utter fear painting her features, but Casey was moving so fast she didn't notice. Jack moved to the child's side. "Come on Chloe, let's get you packed." He reached to the floor by the wall and retrieved her backpack, then started putting her papers and book inside, pushing aside his sling and gritting his teeth against the pain. "Did you get very far on your essay?"

Chloe didn't answer and remained frozen, so Jack kept packing. "No problem if you didn't. You'll have more time when we get somewhere safe, okay?"

Casey ran out the back door and threw their things into the trunk, then returned in a rush to Chloe's side. "I know this is scary, Chloe, but we can't stay here any longer. Those men are probably harmless, but we just can't take that chance."

Chloe finally looked at Casey and met her eye. "Where will we go?"

"I haven't gotten that quite worked out yet, but for now, let's get in the car and get out of sight."

"I'm scared," Chloe said, her whole body trembling.

"I know," Casey soothed. "Here, I'll help you."

A knock at the door startled them all and Casey grabbed Chloe, pulled her up to her feet and headed out the back. Jack followed behind, his gun drawn and pointed toward the living room and the front entrance.

"Ma'am?" Stevens's voice sounded from the front. "Anybody home?"

A cry issued from Chloe's lips, loud enough that the knocking became more insistent.

"Ma'am? FBI! I need you to open this door right now!" They could hear the man kicking at the door and it made them move even faster out the back and down the steps.

Jack was the last to exit. He pulled the door closed behind him and locked it, then dragged over some firewood from nearby to block it. He had only moved a few pieces before he heard the lock at the front door give way and Stevens enter the living room. Jack abandoned the logs and rushed down the steps.

"Mitchell!" Stevens yelled, apparently seeing his quarry through the back door's window. "Stop where you are!"

Casey had gotten Chloe in the backseat and was just closing the door as Jack approached, limping heavily as the strain sent sharp pains through each of his wounds. He met her eye across the top of the car.

"You drive," he said forcefully. "Go down the mountain as fast as you can and don't stop until you lose these guys." He opened the passenger door and barely got it closed behind him before

Casey had the car in motion. It wasn't a moment too soon.

"Mitchell!" Stevens yelled again. "Freeze!"

Jack turned to see Stevens come out on the back porch, stumble over the wood then right himself and fire at the car. The first shot hit the passenger door panel and ripped a hole near the handle, and the second flew wild. Casey gunned the engine and the rear tires spun, then caught, sending the vehicle racing around the cabin and skidding across the rocks in the driveway. As they came around the front of the building, they saw Fletcher running down the porch steps, his gun drawn.

"Get down!" Jack yelled. He already had his window rolled down and he fired at Fletcher, causing the man to jump off the last step and take refuge behind the car. Jack fired another two rounds, this time hitting the front and rear tires of the vehicle. He smiled in grim satisfaction as the bullets ripped into the rubber and both tires exploded.

Casey hit the accelerator again and they sped down the dirt road, leaving their enemies behind them in a large plume of dust. She didn't slow down until they were a good ten minutes away from the cabin.

Jack kept looking behind them, but finally was convinced that no one was following. He stretched to roll up his window and then looked over at Casey. Her face was determined, yet there was ample fear painted there, as well.

"You did great," he praised, putting the safety on his weapon. He turned to Chloe, who was scrunched up against the seat. "How are you doing back there?"

Chloe looked up and he saw fear in her eyes. "I'm okay, I guess. Are they still chasing us?"

"No. I shot out two of their tires, so they're going to have to fix both of them before they can even leave the cabin. They probably only have one spare tire in their trunk, so they'll be stuck there for a while."

The child breathed a sigh of relief. "That's good. Those men are scary."

Casey glanced over at him, then put her eyes back on the road. "They almost killed us!"

"Almost is the key word here," Jack said softly.

Casey looked over again long enough to glare at him. "You think this is funny? Some sort of game? My niece has seen enough! Do you hear me? She doesn't need this—and neither do I!"

Jack instantly sobered. "Sorry. I guess trying to find some humor in all of this is the way I deal with it. Look, this is all my fault. If you just drop me off at the nearest hospital, I'll take it from there. You shouldn't have to be in danger because of me." He grimaced and moved slightly, trying to ease the pain in his side. He looked down and saw a new patch of blood soaking his shirt.

Casey noticed the blood, as well. She quickly pulled the car to the side of the road and stopped, then leaned over and pulled his shirt back. "Oh, Jack, you ripped open your wound, and you're as white as a sheet."

"Yeah, I hit the handrail pretty hard back there when I was going down the stairs." He leaned back to give her better access. Now that the adrenaline rush was over, he realized just how much that last episode had cost him physically. He gripped the car door and scowled as pain shot through him again. "Sorry. I didn't mean to mess up your handiwork."

She touched his face softly and he looked into her eyes. He saw concern there, but also something more that she quickly masked.

Her skin was sweet and warm and he leaned into her touch, enjoying the contact more than he would like to admit. Why was she affecting him this way? After Jaime had died, he had believed he would never fall in love with anyone ever again, yet here he was, drawn to this beautiful lady with the suspicious past. He tamped down the emotions and pulled back slightly. He didn't want those feelings to surface again for anybody. It wasn't worth the pain that inevitably followed.

Casey's hand started to shake and she quickly withdrew it, then turned abruptly toward the backseat. "Chloe, are you sure you're doing okay?"

The girl nodded. "Yes, Aunt Casey." She motioned to Jack. "Is Agent Mitchell going to be okay?"

Casey smiled at her. "Yes, although I'm going to have to stitch him up again."

"It sure was close up there at the cabin, wasn't it?"

"Yep. Way too close for my comfort." She leaned down and pulled the lever that popped open the trunk, keeping her shaking hands out of sight as much as possible. "Hop out and get my medical bag out of the trunk, okay, sweetie?"

A moment later she had Jack pressing a compress on his wound. "Can you hold on to this?" She adjusted it slightly and moved his hand to secure it in place. "Put a little pressure on it to stop the bleeding. That's right. For now I just want to get a little farther down the mountain and hidden somewhere, and then as soon as we're safe, I'll take care of your injuries."

"I think we should keep going, too, but just so you know, we're probably safe for now. Those guys were on their own, and I seriously doubt they had two spare tires."

"I'd rather not find out," Casey answered, her face still flushed. She gripped the steering wheel, appearing embarrassed at her hands still shaking, then put the car in gear and started back down the road, constantly glancing out the rearview mirror just in case.

# SEVEN

Casey and Jack rode in silence for a few minutes as Jack mulled over the attack at the cabin. Stevens and Fletcher had been by themselves without any local backup, which meant they were still trying to take care of their loose end on their own. Jack hoped that was a good sign, but he wouldn't be sure until he talked to someone in the FBI field office. Either way, he didn't want Casey and Chloe to get caught in the middle of another firefight.

"Look," Jack said quietly. "I meant what I said about the hospital. I don't want you two in danger anymore because of me. If you don't mind, just take me to the nearest hospital and drop me off. I'll figure something out from there."

Casey gave him a look like he was crazed. When she spoke, her voice was tinged with anger. "Okay, Jack, let's think about your plan," she said roughly. "Doing what you suggest would be a death sentence for you. First of all, you're severely injured and you need to rest. If you don't, you're not going to be able to defend yourself when they come after you again. Do you really think you'll be able to rest in the hospital, especially if they arrest you once they find out who you are? And what makes you think Stevens and Fletcher won't try to kill you in the hospital? They sure didn't have any qualms about coming up and shooting up the cabin, and the hospital is filled with innocent people that could get caught up in the crossfire."

"I just don't want you and Chloe mixed up in this anymore," Jack said forcefully. "I don't want the two of you hurt because of me."

"It's a little too late for that." Casey's voice was firm, as well. "I appreciate the thought, but let's be realistic. You think those two guys are just going to forget they saw us? Stevens isn't some local wet-behind-the-ears security guard. He's with the FBI, and I bet he's just as tenacious as you are! As soon as they get to a phone he'll probably have an all-points bulletin out on my car with our full descriptions. I put mud all over the license plate, but that won't slow them down for long. You think they won't have guards at the hospital within the hour, waiting for our arrival with open arms?" The car skidded a little on the dirt, and she slowed but kept moving forward.

Jack scowled, still in pain and frustrated on top of it. "I don't know what to think. Seems to me like they're trying to take me out without getting any other law enforcement involved, but you're right. If I were at a hospital, I'd be in danger and could be a danger to others, at least until I can prove what really happened out there in the woods." He closed his eyes. "I need to call my office and start getting this sorted out. They have to be looking for me, but Stevens might have already convinced them all that I'm a murderer."

"There's no consistent cell service anywhere around here. Do you want to try using a pay phone?"

"Do any of those still exist?"

Casey shrugged. "Who knows? Maybe I should just buy you a throwaway cell and we can go farther down the mountain until we get within range of a tower. Then you can call and get this whole thing figured out."

Jack opened his eyes and looked at her intently. "Well, first things first. We need a hotel room or somewhere else we can stay that's off the beaten path. Any new thoughts?" They'd already spent some time discussing places where they could go once Stevens came back. As of their last discussion, she hadn't had any ideas. He could only hope something new had occurred to her since then.

"I realized the other day that we're at the edge of the Uwharrie National Forest. Why don't we find a phone, then head back up into the forest and stay at one of the cabins in the national park? The park service probably has a few available and they should be pretty cheap, not to mention secluded. Maybe there we can regroup."

Jack leaned back and closed his eyes. The exertion had worn him out, and with even the slightest movement he acutely felt every injury that he had sustained. "Sounds like a plan. Stevens will probably assume that we're headed back for Charlotte. I doubt he'll even think to look at the national park. Let me know when you come across a phone or a place that sells them. We'll go on from there."

About half an hour later, Casey pulled into a gas station with a food mart at the outskirts of a small town. Chloe was sleeping peacefully in the backseat and Casey leaned back and put a blanket over her, then looked at Jack in the front seat. He had also fallen asleep, but it seemed far from peaceful. She could see stress lines from the pain, and his face was still pale. She knew he had not healed nearly enough to be gallivanting around the countryside in his current condition. Still, they had no choice, and because of Jack they had been able to escape the men back at the cabin. She touched his cheek lightly and felt the bristles of his beard against her fingers.

Medical school had left zero time for dating, but even so, she had never felt her heart race like it did whenever Jack Mitchell was nearby. She had done her best to avoid him at the cabin, but she had never been able to eliminate the feelings of attraction that kept springing up whenever he touched her.

She laughed to herself and withdrew her hand. There was no way a relationship with Jack would ever work anyway, so there was no use wasting time thinking about the impossible. Despite the attraction she felt, Jack Mitchell was an FBI agent, and she was so afraid of law enforcement that she wouldn't even tell him her last name. Still, with all of the stress and turmoil in her life, it was nice to dream about what could have been if she had met Jack under different circumstances in another time and place.

She moved her hand to his arm. "Jack? Wake up, Jack. We're at a gas station and they actually have a pay phone."

Jack stirred and looked around the car, taking a moment to return to the here and now. He looked over at Casey. "Hello, Princess. Was I out long?"

Casey smiled. "About half an hour. Feel better?"

"A little." He pulled back the bandage that was covering his abdominal wound and looked at the blood on the gauze. It had stopped bleeding, but the skin was a mess where he had torn up the wound. He had been moving so fast coming out of the cabin that he hadn't realized how hard he had hit the railing. "Do you have any more of that pain medicine you gave me before?"

"Sure thing. I'll go inside and buy you some juice and crackers or something while you make your call. You can eat something and take the meds when you get back."

Jack nodded, then opened the door and headed toward the phone. He wasn't sure what to expect when he called, but the call had to be made. He put some coins in the slot, then dialed the number for Ben Lennox, one of the FBI agents that he counted as a true friend. Ben was familiar with the conspiracy investigation, and he trusted Ben above all others to help him figure this whole thing out.

Ben answered on the third ring.

"Lennox, Federal Bureau of Investigation."

"It's Jack, Ben. Can you talk?"

There was a pause, then Ben was back. "Call me on my cell in five minutes. I'll get out of the building."

A few minutes later they were reconnected. "Jack, you're hot, man. Where are you?"

"It's a long story, Ben. I was following a lead on the conspiracy case when I got double-crossed. Brett Stevens shot me and left me for dead. I've been trying to recuperate enough to call in."

"Unbelievable." Ben paused. "Did you know you're wanted for murder? We've got people watching all of the airports, train and bus stations, and your credit cards and bank accounts have all been tagged. D.A. Colby just called and threatened the chief. He's already talking about convening a grand jury. For all I know he's got taps on the Bureau phones in his quest to find and prosecute you."

"I caught a snippet of a news story," Jack answered. "I know that Denton's body was found in the trunk of my car. What do you know that the reporters aren't saying?"

"Forensics discovered your bullet in Denton's chest."

"Look, Ben, I did kill him, but it was self-defense, and I sure didn't put him in my trunk. Stevens is trying to frame me, and he's working with another guy named Fletcher. Check the forensics report if you need more proof. They had to have found something that points to Stevens or Fletcher. They're the ones that must have moved the body. You should take a crime-scene team up to the mountains, too, just south of Denton's cabin. It's been almost two weeks, so the crime scene is hardly pristine, but I can't imagine all of that blood is gone yet. A good team might be able to find other evidence, too."

"What happened up there, Jack?"

"I got a warrant to check out Denton's cabin and as soon as I left, Stevens showed up with Denton and Fletcher and started shooting. Before Stevens tried to finish me off, he admitted his role in the conspiracy. We need to run a check on his financials. He said he got involved in the ring to pay off gambling debts. He's dirty, Ben. He tried to kill me."

Ben paused, taking it all in. "You said you got shot. Are you okay?"

"I got hit four times, but I'm mending. It'll take a while, though, before I'm back to one hundred percent."

"Do you have any proof? Any witnesses? I trust you, Jack, but you know it's going to take more than that to clean this mess up."

Jack didn't want to mention Casey until he had a handle on what she had really seen—and who she really was. For now he left her out of the equation. "Fletcher saw him shoot me, but he's on Colby's payroll, too. I doubt he'll tell the truth unless we offer him some sort of deal. I do have Stevens's bullet that got dug out of my shoulder."

Ben was quiet for a minute. "That bullet won't be enough to get you off the hook here. Stevens claimed you discovered evidence at Denton's cabin that implicated you, and that you killed Denton and then shot at him and disappeared with the evidence. He admitted shooting you, but claims it was self-defense, and the D.A. is buying his story."

Jack grimaced. "That's not a surprise. If I'm dead, I'm an easy pawn to blame, and the investigation comes to a standstill. Then Colby and his crew can keep selling verdicts." He combed his hair with his fingers. "I did pick up a laptop and some papers at Denton's, but I never had a chance to really look at them. Stevens grabbed them after he shot me and I need to find them. Do you think he still has them anywhere?"

"I doubt it," Ben answered. "If there's anything noted inside that implicates him or Colby, he'd be a fool to keep them."

Jack hit the phone booth with his fist. "It's no wonder the D.A. is moving forward to take me out of the picture. He's in league with Stevens. They've been fixing the cases together for a couple of years now and making a good profit to boot. If he can kill me outright, or at least blame me for Denton's death, he can take me out of the picture and discredit any evidence I find against him. They can't get away with this."

"We need more than just your word if we're going to stop them," Lennox said thoughtfully. Then he added, "How about this—one of the big keys to this puzzle is the log at the evidence storage room. You and I both know those logs were altered in the Simpson case, but I just don't have the techno savvy to prove it. I've got a buddy that works up at the Regional Computer Forensics Laboratory. He can do wonders with the FBI server and find things people think they've deleted forever. Right after you disappeared I sent him the files and asked him to take a look at the logs, kinda on the side."

"Does the chief know?" Jack trusted his boss, but with Stevens being dirty, and D.A. Colby having a very long reach, he didn't want anyone else involved until they had proof.

"Not yet. My friend says he's making progress and needs a few more days. It sounds like that's the only chance we have of backing up your story and proving your innocence. Can you stay off the radar that long? If you get arrested before he can come up with something, Colby and Stevens might try to eliminate you while you're in custody. Your life is definitely still in danger. If you do manage to survive, even the chief won't be able to protect you against the indictment after you're taken into custody without some kind of evidence against Colby and Stevens."

Jack thought about that. He was honest enough with himself to know that he would struggle in his present physical condition without Casey's help, but he didn't want to put her in any more danger, either. Would she stay if she knew the truth? Was it even fair to ask her? He was definitely in a quandary.

"I'll figure something out. I don't have a cell

phone right now to call you, but I'll try to work out a way to get in touch with you in two days for an update. Sound like a plan?"

"Good," Ben agreed. "Call me in two days and I'll let you know where we stand."

Jack blew out a breath. "Look, Ben. I know you're going out on a limb for me here. I appreciate it."

"Jack, if what you're saying is true, we need to stop this conspiracy before it goes any further. I want Colby and Stevens behind bars just like you do. Period. It's worth waiting a couple of days to make sure this gets done right and you don't get killed in the process."

"Mendoza will be livid if you don't tell him what's going on."

"It'll be worth the reprimand if we can stop those two. We'll get the evidence we need, and then we'll tell Mendoza and put an end to this madness. Stay safe, and call me in two days. Got it?"

Jack looked back over to the car where Casey was just hanging up the gas pump. "Ben, I have another favor to ask."

"Shoot."

"Look, I know you're already putting your job on the line by helping me under the radar, but I need to know some information not connected to the conspiracy case. I want to see what you can find about a woman named Casey out of Florida. She's got medical training and seems to be on the run with a girl about ten years old named Chloe."

"Last names?" Ben asked.

Jack kept his eyes on Casey. "I'm not sure. I do know she's in her late twenties and about five foot eight with brown hair and blue eyes. The little girl has blue eyes and blond hair, and is around four feet tall. Average builds for both of them. Anything you can tell me would be helpful."

"You got it. I'll see what I can find and let you know the next time we talk."

"Deal." Jack hung up, keeping his eye on Casey. He felt a strange mixture of emotions about his "princess." He wanted to know the truth, but at the same time, he was afraid that the facts he was searching for would open an entire Pandora's box of questions—one that Casey would do anything to keep closed.

# EIGHT

Jack limped back over to the car where Casey was putting the cap back on the gas tank and gave her a nod. "Everything okay?"

Casey nodded. "Yeah. Chloe's in the bathroom. You get anything worked out?"

He shrugged. "Some. I need to stay hidden for a little while longer. Those charges we saw on the TV are real and I still need some time to prove my innocence. I've got a buddy helping me on the inside, but it's going to take a few more days to get the evidence we need. Maybe you can drop me at the first motel we come across and then get out of this mess."

Casey shook her head. "No, that's not going to happen. Look, Jack. I've got to stitch you back up and then you're going to rest and recuperate and you're not going to do it alone. Got it?"

Jack gave a small smile at her tone. She was a

bulldog when she wanted to be, but he could be just as tenacious. "I meant it when I said I don't want you or Chloe hurt because of me. These guys aren't going to stop until I'm dead. I know too much. You could end up right in the line of fire again."

"I'm not changing my mind," she replied, her arms crossed.

Jack couldn't help himself. He leaned forward and kissed her right on the lips. "You're incredible. Do you know that?"

Casey looked surprised, but recovered quickly as soon as Chloe came out of the store and got in the backseat of the car. Casey locked eyes with Jack for a moment but Jack quickly looked away, regretting his impulsive move. Why had he done that? It wasn't fair to lead her on. Even though he had feelings for her, there was no way he could act on them given the circumstances.

She reached out and handed Jack two pills and a package of crackers. Jack took them quickly, thankful that she didn't mention the kiss. "There's a soda for you in the cup holder. These will help with the pain."

He nodded gratefully, but staggered as he moved to get back in the car. He'd been on his feet way too much today. Casey quickly got under his arm and helped him get in the front seat, then closed the door behind him. He watched her every move as she circled the car and came around to the driver's side, then once again got behind the wheel.

"Thank you, Princess. I really do appreciate everything you're doing for me."

She turned to him and gave him a tentative smile. "You're welcome. Rest, okay?"

About a half an hour later, Casey pulled into the ranger station at the national park. Jack was asleep again, aided in part by the medication he had taken. She looked back at Chloe and gave her a wink.

"You doing okay back there?"

Chloe nodded. "You bet, Aunt Casey."

Casey rubbed her forehead. "Good. You stay here and keep an eye on Jack, and I'll go take care of getting us a cabin. Deal?"

Chloe nodded and Casey glanced over at the FBI agent. He was still pale and Casey was glad that he was getting some of the rest he needed. There were small lines around his eyes and mouth that testified to the pain he had suffered, and dark circles under his eyes. The stubble on his face seemed to make him even rougher around the edges, and she felt her heart squeeze as she said a silent prayer for his condition. What he needed was time to actually recuperate from his injuries in a proper medical facility, not to go driving across the countryside. Hopefully the national-park cabins would be far enough off the beaten path to give them all time to regroup and figure out what to do next.

She pulled herself out of the car and walked up to the ranger station. She was met by a ranger with dark hair and friendly features working behind a desk. He had a small color TV on behind him but didn't seem to be paying much attention to it as he read through a stack of papers. He looked up and smiled at her as she approached.

"Afternoon, ma'am. Can I help you?"

Casey smiled in return. "I sure hope so. I'm interested in renting one of your cabins for a week. Do you have anything available?"

He pulled out a paper map and circled one of the buildings depicted in the middle of the diagram. "I sure do. This is the ranger station here, and we have these three cabins empty right now. These two have two bedrooms, and this one just has one." He circled some more buildings, then looked up expectantly.

Casey studied the map, then made her choice.

"This one looks good." Hoping to sound like a normal visitor, she added, "Any good hiking trails around? I'd like to get some exercise in while I'm up here. I love to hike."

The ranger nodded and pulled out another brochure that advertised the features of the national park and circled the hiking section that described several of the trails.

Suddenly Casey's heart sped into overdrive and she could barely breathe. A picture of her car—including the exact make, model and color—flashed on the TV, right behind the ranger. She couldn't quite hear the newsman's words, but the next thing she knew, Jack's picture was on the screen and a headline reading Missing was painted in large black letters across the top.

"Ma'am? How did you want to pay for this?"

Casey started as the ranger's words broke through her thoughts. He must have noticed the change in her because he suddenly looked worried. "Are you all right?"

Casey nodded quickly. "Yes, sorry." She gave him a reassuring smile. "I'm just a little tired from a very long week and I think it's finally catching up with me. I might just take a nap before I hit the trails."

The ranger smiled and nodded, still appearing slightly unsure about her, but apparently not wanting to push the issue. "Just fill out this card with your name and address, and the total will be $150. I can take cash or credit card."

Casey put a fake name and address on the registration card, then paid cash for the cabin and pocketed the key the ranger handed out to her.

"I hope you enjoy your stay."

Casey nodded. "Thanks. I'm sure this country air will do me good."

She turned and hurried back to the car, her mind filled with questions. Had the ranger noticed her vehicle when she'd pulled up to book the cabin? Part of her wanted to immediately leave and find a different place to stay, but if her car and Jack's face were plastered on the airwaves, there wouldn't be anywhere else to go that would be any safer. Driving around with him in the car seemed even more foolhardy than staying holed up here in the woods, especially now that people would know to be on the lookout for her car. Besides, their finances were limited, and she'd already paid for the cabin.

A wave of fear shot through her, but she fisted her hands. She would get through this, she coached herself. The ranger probably saw hundreds of cars coming and going from the park. She doubted he would even recognize the type of car she was driving.

A few minutes later she pulled up to her cabin. She and Chloe helped get Jack settled in the smaller bedroom, then got the few supplies they had brought with them unpacked. Chloe made everyone a sandwich while Casey made the beds and did a general inventory of what they needed from the store. They had abandoned their last abode in such a hurry that much had been left behind, and Casey knew she also had to restock her supply of bandages and a few other easily acquired items for her medical bag.

Once Chloe finished making the sandwiches, Casey took one and a bottle of juice and headed to Jack's room. She knocked softly on his door and went in when he answered.

"How are you doing?"

"I feel like I just got run over by a truck." He smiled at her and it made her stomach flip.

"I thought I'd fix your stitches and then you could have something to eat. Are you hungry?"

He shrugged but motioned her forward. "A little, I guess." He winced as he pushed himself up on his elbows.

She went to his side and set the meal down

on the end table as he pulled his shirt out of the way to give her better access. She gave him a local anesthetic, cleaned the wound then removed what was left of the old stitches and replaced them with new ones. His skin was cool to the touch and her fingers actually tingled from the contact as she worked. When she looked up, his eyes were intensely watching her every move.

"You sure are good at this."

"I'm sorry it's necessary. You must be exhausted." She finished bandaging the wound, then started putting her supplies back in the bag. He grabbed her hands and stopped her as a sudden warmth spread throughout her arms and squeezed her heart.

"Thank you, Casey. I still can't figure you out, but I know you're sacrificing a lot for me. Most people would have just left me lying out there in the woods. You've gone way beyond the call of duty."

Their eyes locked and Casey seemed unable to pull away. His eyes were dark and mesmerizing.

"I just did what anybody would have done...."

"That's not true." Jack countered, his thumb gently caressing the back of her hand. "You really are a princess, you know that? Your friendship through all of this has meant so much to me."

The words were like a splash of cold water, clearing her head and reminding her of what Jack clearly already knew—there couldn't be anything between them but friendship. Even that was pushing it. A romantic relationship certainly wouldn't be possible. He was still mourning his late wife, and she was still running from a past that had her at odds with the law—and with FBI agents like Jack.

"You don't even know me," she protested, pulling her hands away. "I've made a lot of mistakes in my life."

"I can see your heart," he responded. "That's enough." He closed his eyes.

Casey knew the medicine he'd taken had made him drowsy, and he had been weak to start with even before the afternoon chase. It was no wonder he was so tired. What he needed were a few uninterrupted weeks to recuperate, but she doubted he would be able to get that rest with two killers on his trail and the press constantly publicizing his photo. She sure hoped the national park would be a haven of safety for them for at least a few days while she tried to figure out her next move.

She zipped up her medical bag and covered Jack with a blanket, then closed the door softly behind her. Chloe had already started a fire in the stone fireplace and was warming herself by the flames when Casey returned to the living room.

"Is Agent Mitchell okay, Aunt Casey?"

Casey nodded. "Yeah. He's almost asleep." She came up and gave her niece a hug. "You did terrific, you know? It was scary back there at the cabin, but you were great. I'm really proud of you."

Chloe accepted the praise, but her face was still troubled. "Where are we going to live now? We can't stay here forever."

"No, we can't," Casey replied. "But God will help us figure something out. We can't give up just because the going gets tough."

"Is it always gonna be like this? I mean, running from place to place with somebody chasing us?"

"I don't know, Chloe. I sure hope not. Sometimes we just have to take each day as it comes. God's mercies are new every morning, though. I do know that."

"Okay." The little girl nodded, then reached for her backpack. "I'm going to read a little bit, unless you want me to do something else."

Casey shook her head and tugged the girl's

pigtail playfully. Chloe was an excellent reader, and she knew her niece often escaped into the pages of a good book when times were stressful. "No, go ahead. I'm going to sit down and rest myself." She sank down wearily into the couch and touched her lips in a thoughtless motion. Now that Jack and Chloe were taken care of, she finally had a moment to really think about what had happened.

Jack had kissed her back at the convenience store. He had actually kissed her. She had been so stunned when it happened that she hadn't even had time to react. Just as well, given how quick he'd been to remind her that they were nothing more than friends.

She turned her thoughts to her current dilemma. Chloe's father was searching for them and had reported Chloe's disappearance to the police, so she was sure she could never return to Florida or even Georgia without having to constantly look over her shoulder. She doubted the other states were as vigilant about searching for her since they had their own criminals to worry about, but she just couldn't afford to take any chances.

If Chloe's father ever caught up to them, she was sure that Chloe's life would be in danger, as well as her own. Sure, he would play the grieving widower who had been wronged to the press, but as soon as he was no longer under the spotlight, the control and abuse he'd used to victimize his wife would begin for Chloe. He would also never let Casey's actions go unpunished. Casey had dared to defy him, and when her sister had done that, it had cost her her life.

Casey shivered. She felt like a net was closing in around her. Where could she take Chloe and be safe? Her money was running low, but finding a job that paid under the table would be difficult, as well. How could she find a cheap *and* safe place to go? The cabin in the mountains had been the perfect solution, but that option was off the table now.

She ran her hands through her hair and sighed. God's mercies were new every morning, just like she had told Chloe, so she would take each day as it came and try not to worry about the future. Somehow God would help her find a new place to live with her niece where they would be safe. She glanced around the simple yet comfortable living room. The cabin where they were staying now was comparatively cheap, but it wasn't a long-term solution to her problem. She rolled over all of the different options she could think of. Where could she go? And how could she stay safe now that not only Chloe's father but Stevens and Fletcher appeared to be after her, too?

# NINE

The screen door squeaked loudly and made Jack stir from his nap. He blinked a couple of times and wiped his eyes, then took in his surroundings. By the light coming in through the window, he guessed he had slept an entire night away. He wasn't sure, but it felt like it was about eight or so in the morning.

He listened for a moment and heard a floorboard groan. That was odd. He couldn't put his finger on what was wrong, but a sliver of apprehension shot down his spine. He pulled himself up to a sitting position, scowling at the effort it took. Suddenly his door opened and he froze when he saw the pistol pointed directly at his head.

"Well, well, Jack. It seems like you do have nine lives. I guess I killed you too quickly last time. Believe me, I won't make the same mistake again."

Jack's eyes narrowed as he glared at his former partner, but Stevens barely seemed to notice. He motioned with his gun. "Get up. Now."

"What did you do with the evidence I got from Denton's?" Jack asked, not moving from his current position. Stalling was the only tactic he could think of at this point. There was no place to go—no escape possible. The best he could hope for would be to delay Stevens long enough to come up with a plan, or seize an unexpected opportunity.

The attempt didn't work.

"I said, get up now," Stevens ordered roughly. He came closer to Jack and grabbed his bad arm, yanking him from the bed.

The pain from his shoulder wound shot through Jack's entire torso, and he swallowed a howl of agony. He balled his good hand into a fist and swung at Stevens, hoping to hit the man's jaw and force him to release his arm. Wounded and in his present condition, however, Jack was no match for the other agent's strength. Not only did Stevens easily avoid the blow, but he used Jack's lunge against him to hit the butt of his pistol against the side of Jack's head.

Lights flashed before Jack's eyes as he went down on the floor, but he had just enough presence of mind left to try to protect his wounds by curling into a ball. Stevens pulled back, then gave him a vicious kick that made Jack cry out in anguish.

"Now this is what's going to happen, Jack. You're going to get up, and you're not going to give me any more trouble, got it? Then you're going to come with me out to my car, and we're going to take a little ride. Understand?"

Jack felt a wave of nausea sweep over him and he wondered for a minute if he could even make it outside. "How…how did you find me?" he asked softly, his voice barely audible. This time, the stalling technique worked.

"Your car," Stevens answered smugly. "I had Fletcher call in an anonymous tip about what car your girlfriend was driving, and the FBI added the make and model to your BOLO that's running on all of the news stations. A park-ranger friend of mine recognized the car when your girlfriend registered for the cabin. He gave me a friendly call, so here I am."

Jack moved slightly, and then winced as another pain shot through him. He'd seen the original "be on the lookout" story on the news but wasn't aware that they'd updated the report. He wanted to deny that Casey was his girlfriend, but at the same time, he didn't want to bring her into the conversation. Hopefully she and Chloe were safely hidden somewhere away from this maniac with the gun. He tried stalling again, hoping that if she was nearby, she'd have ample time to get away.

"You can still stop before this goes too far, Brett. You used to be a good cop. I'll help you. I promise I'll do whatever I can."

Stevens laughed, but there was no mirth in his voice; instead it was tinged with bitterness. "I'm way past the point of no return, partner. Colby has made it perfectly clear that if I don't take care of you, he will. In fact, he's also made it clear that if I don't take care of you soon, I'll share your fate. I'm out of choices."

"You always have a choice."

"Not this time. I'm losing my patience, Jack. Get up now."

Jack put up his hands in a motion of surrender, then gradually managed to get on his hands and knees. Slowly he got to his feet, then suddenly charged at Stevens, hitting the other man as hard as he could in the midriff.

Stevens was surprised by the attack and the

gun went flying as the two men hit the wall hard. He reacted quickly, though, by bringing both of his hands together and driving them forcefully into Jack's back in a devastating blow. Jack fell to the ground and Stevens leaned over him and pulled his arms roughly behind him to handcuff him, ignoring the groan of pain Jack uttered as he did so. Then Stevens stepped over Jack and retrieved the gun that had landed a few feet away.

"You just won't give up, will you, Jack? Don't you know when you've lost the game?"

Jack was breathing hard, trying to recover from the agony he was feeling. Nausea swept over him once again and he had to focus hard just to stay conscious. He groaned again as Stevens pulled him to his feet once more. This time he knew he was too weak to put up more of a fight, especially with his hands cuffed behind him. He glared at Stevens, but didn't have the strength to even answer him.

Stevens pushed him out the door and into the hallway. Jack surveyed the front room, hoping Casey and Chloe were nowhere around. Stevens apparently hadn't seen them—Jack was sure that if they'd been around when Stevens had entered the cabin, his former partner would have pointed the gun at Casey instead of Jack to ensure Jack's compliance. Their absence gave him hope that maybe they had a chance of escape if they could stay out of this madman's way.

Stevens pushed him again toward the front door and Jack stumbled, then fell hard against the side of the couch. His head was still spinning and blood was getting in his right eye from the new head wound, making it hard to see.

"You don't look like much of a Boy Scout now, do you, Jack? You were always so perfect, always the shining star at the Bureau. But now they think you're a murderer. Did you know that? I put Denton's body in your trunk at your apartment, and the D.A. is ready to prosecute." He leaned closer. "I'm going to kill you, Jack, and they'll never find your body. They'll always think you were guilty, and your reputation will always be in shreds, even long after you're gone." Stevens hauled Jack to his feet one more time, then pulled him out the front door and down the steps.

Jack looked around the best he could, expecting to see Stevens's new accomplice Fletcher somewhere. He saw no one.

"Where's your new partner?"

"Busy. But don't worry. I'll let him know when you're dead."

Suddenly Jack heard a thump behind him, followed by a soft moan. He turned to see Stevens's eyes glaze over, then watched as his body slowly slumped to the ground. Behind him stood Casey, holding a large piece of wood in her hands, her eyes wide and looking like a startled deer.

His princess had saved him again.

Casey's hands started shaking and she dropped the piece of wood and took a step back. A moment later the shock of what she'd done seemed to wear off and she rushed to Jack's side and gently wiped the blood away from his eyes. "Are you okay? Oh, my! Look at what that man did to you!"

"I'll be okay," Jack answered, his voice rough. "Can you find his handcuff key? It should be in his pocket."

Casey moved to the fallen man. First, she verified he had a pulse, then she struggled to roll him over. Finally she succeeded and checked his breathing before checking his pockets until she came up with the key. Quickly she hurried back over to Jack and removed the handcuffs. Jack took them from her, along with the key, then went to Stevens and handcuffed him. He also secured the man's weapon. Then he turned and enveloped Casey into a large hug.

"Thank you. You saved my life again. He

would have killed me for sure. Your timing is amazing." He pulled back and looked into her eyes, which were still wide with fear. He imagined it had been hard for her to attack Stevens, especially since the man could have easily turned and shot her if he'd heard her approach. "Is Chloe safe?"

Casey nodded. "She's waiting in the car down the road. We need to hurry and get back to her, but I want to grab a few things from the cabin before we go." She reached up and touched his face gently, examining his new wound. "What did that man do to you?"

Jack released her and stepped back. "I'll be okay eventually. At least he didn't shoot me this time, though I'm sure the thought crossed his mind. We'd better hurry. He won't stay out very long." He touched her back lightly, then staggered as dizziness overcame him. She quickly moved under his arm for support and helped him regain his balance. Then together they slowly moved back to the cabin door and inside the living room.

Casey led Jack to the couch to sit down, and then she hurried to gather their things. He could hear her moving swiftly from room to room and wanted to help her, but he couldn't seem to get his body to work the way he intended it to. Frustration swept over him, and he raised his hand and wiped more blood away from his eyes. Three times he'd evaded death at Stevens's hands, but each encounter brought additional injuries and no new advances on cracking the case.

Should he throw in the towel and call the Bureau now? If he did, would he be arrested as a murderer? Sure, Stevens had confessed, but at this point it was still one man's word against the other's without any corroborating evidence. Stevens would deny everything and just claim that Jack had resisted arrest so he'd had to subdue him, both here and at Casey's cabin.

He thought about Casey. Where had she been while Stevens was taking him out of the cabin? Had she been close enough to hear his ex-partner's latest confession? His mind went back to the first attack on him in the forest. Had she seen the initial shooting? She still hadn't admitted to it, but Jack felt certain that she knew more than she was telling. If he could just convince her to tell her side of the story, Stevens could get arrested today. Why was she holding back? He winced as pain shot through him, but he pushed the feelings aside as best he could and rose again to his feet by sheer force of will.

"Casey?"

Casey appeared, holding a tote bag. "Why are you up? I'm almost done. Just give me a couple more minutes." She moved forward and handed him the tote bag that contained his gun, wallet and other belongings, then tried to get him to sit back down on the couch.

"Casey, wait. We should call the police. We can tell them what happened at your cabin yesterday, and you can tell them about when I got shot. Stevens will get arrested and this whole thing can be over right now."

Casey took a step back, then another, her eyes wide and instantly fearful. "I can't do that, Jack." She looked at the tote bag, and he could see her mind spinning. She was obviously aware that she had just given him his weapon. Was she afraid he would use his gun to force her to comply? The idea seemed ridiculous, yet there was panic in her eyes. What was it that had her so scared?

A flash of frustration filled him. "Can't, or won't?"

"Both. It's the same thing."

A moment passed, then another, as their eyes locked. Jack noticed that she didn't deny that she'd seen the shooting. She was just refusing to testify, and without her testimony, Jack had nothing concrete to prove his innocence or Stevens's guilt. If he called the FBI now without her on board, he would go to jail, and Stevens and Colby would quash whatever evidence still existed, if any, to ensure his conviction.

And while that was happening, Casey would have to deal with the authorities he brought in. She'd have to face whatever it was that happened in Florida that had left her running scared. Could he really do that to her when he still had no idea what she was up against, no way to help her or shield her from some of the consequences of her actions?

He glanced back up at Casey, who had taken another step backward. She looked incredibly vulnerable, and her expression squeezed his heart. He still didn't know her story, but she had just saved his life. Again. From a man who would, without hesitation, take any chance to hurt her for getting in his way. She could have left him or even let Stevens take him, but she had stood her ground, and for that he was extremely thankful.

Jack made a decision. He would figure out her history and the cause of her reticence at some point, but for now he'd have to think of something else. He held up his hands in mock surrender. "Okay, Casey, okay. Forget I mentioned it. Let's just get out of here."

Casey didn't move for a moment and looked as if she was gauging his truthfulness. Then, finally, she nodded and went back to collecting their things. A few minutes later she was by his side again, a backpack slung over her shoulder, a suitcase in each hand and her medical bag tucked under her arm. Jack was able to walk by himself this time, but he was glad that she was staying close anyway, just in case.

He followed her out the back door and through the woods toward her car, catching a small glimpse of Stevens, who was still lying on the ground and just starting to come to.

"Oh, man, that hurts." Jack groaned as he stumbled, but Casey was quick to support him and get him moving again. As they approached the car, Chloe saw them coming and jumped out to grab a bag from her aunt's hands and open the door.

"You look awful, Agent Mitchell," she said softly.

Jack gave a small laugh. "I feel awful. It's a set. And like I told you, it's Jack—not Agent Mitchell." Together they got him settled in the front seat of the car. Afterward Chloe helped Casey get the luggage into the trunk. Casey reached for the tote that had his gun, but he shook his head and held fast to the straps.

"The gun stays with me."

She hesitated for a minute, her eyes again locking with his, but she finally shrugged, closed his door and hurried to the driver's seat. A few moments later they were on the road.

"We're going to need to stick to the back roads. My partner added your car's description to the 'be on the lookout' notice for me. They've got police everywhere searching for us and the public has been notified, so anyone we see could potentially put the authorities on our trail."

Casey tensed but nodded at his words. She kept checking her rearview mirror as she drove, but after about ten minutes she seemed to relax a little and her shoulders sagged against the seat.

Jack reached over and touched her arm lightly. "You did the right thing, Casey. He would have killed me for sure. I know it couldn't have been easy for you though. Thank you."

Casey blew out a breath and Jack noticed tears in her eyes. "I'm not in the habit of hitting people. Really, I'm not, but though the whole thing scared me to death, I just couldn't let him take you." She brushed some hair away from her face and he could see that she was trembling.

Jack gave her arm a reassuring squeeze. "Want me to drive?" He knew it was impossible, but he got the desired response. She smiled at him and wiped the tears away.

"Okay, hotshot," she said quietly. "Where to now?"

# TEN

Jack leaned back against the door and wiped his eyes. "I need evidence against Stevens, and right now I have nothing. Remember the satchel I mentioned before? If he still has that somewhere, it might have the information inside that I need to be able to prove that he's a part of this conspiracy."

Casey glanced at him, then put her eyes back on the road. "Well, he'd be just plain stupid to carry something like that around with him. Where would he stash it?"

"If he still has it, I'm thinking it might be at his house. He's not under investigation, so he has no reason to worry about someone coming in with a search warrant. He wouldn't keep something like that at the Bureau, and I doubt it's in his car."

Casey glanced at him again. "Well, why would he keep it at all? Wouldn't he just destroy it?"

Jack shrugged. "You're probably right. He might have saved it for a day or two to make sure there were no references in the files to other pieces of incriminating evidence that he'd need to track down, but odds are he got rid of it. I'm running out of options here though, so I have to at least look and make sure. One way or another, I have to find something that will implicate him. Right now I can't prove my innocence, or his guilt. That satchel is the only lead I can think of for us to pursue." He didn't mention the investigation Lennox had initiated of the evidence room logs. Until he knew what, if anything, would come from it, he had to pin his hopes on the satchel.

Casey glanced at Chloe, who was sitting in the back seat, and Jack saw the girl nod out of the corner of his eye. Apparently they had come to some sort of agreement together, although he wasn't quite sure what to expect from the two.

"Okay, Jack. We're in. Tell me how to get to Stevens's house. If we hurry, maybe we can manage to get there and take a look before he has a chance to set himself free and stop us." She bit her bottom lip. "What are we going to do about the car, though? The police are looking for it right now like you said. They also have your face and the updated information on all of the news shows. Someone's bound to recognize both you and the car sooner or later."

"There's not much we can do about the car. I'd buy us a used junker somewhere if I could, but I found out when I called my friend at the Bureau that they've either frozen my accounts or put tracers on them, so all I have is the money in my wallet. If I use a credit card for anything they'll be able to track us down in no time. As far as my face goes, the best I can do is buy some sunglasses and a hat somewhere." He grinned at her. "Would you mind stitching me up one more time? They may not notice my face from the TV, but anyone that sees us will definitely remember me if I have blood running into my eyes."

Casey smiled. "You think?" She shook her head. "You know, Jack, testing my medical skills is starting to become a habit with you."

Medical skills. Jack filed away that comment away. He was sure Casey had had some medical training, but he was starting to think she was much more than just an EMT or nurse. After all, how many people could perform emergency surgery with almost no equipment in a mountain cabin? The more he thought about it, the more amazing the situation seemed.

Her reaction to his law enforcement suggestion back at the cabin also intrigued him. She had to be running from the law. It was the only idea that made sense. But what could she have done? He knew very few criminals who would go on the lam with their ten-year-old niece in tow, and Chloe seemed to love her aunt and was very devoted to her. Plus, Casey's caring, generous personality and her willingness to help him made her different from any criminal he'd ever known. She was definitely on the run, but she didn't act like a criminal.

Maybe if he could discover her situation and what had made her scared enough to run, he could help her and pay her back for all of the help she had given him. She was clearly in over her head, no matter what was going on. He wished he had access to his FBI computer system so he could satisfy his curiosity, but it would still have to wait. The best he could hope for was to have Lennox fill in some of the blanks when he talked to him again on the phone.

Casey pulled into a convenience store parking lot in front of some side bathrooms. She jumped out and soon came back with some wet paper towels and a small bag of ice. She got back into the car and gingerly wiped away the bulk of the blood from Jack's head wound, then used her medical supplies to clean the wound and stitch it closed while Chloe made him an ice pack out of one of her spare T-shirts.

With that injury taken care of, he was in as good shape as he could get. He was bruised up from the rest of Stevens's assault, but there was nothing more Casey could do for him besides offer him some more pain medication. He refused the stronger painkillers to avoid the sleepy side effects, but he took two aspirin to at least take the edge off what he was feeling. Casey verified that Stevens hadn't managed to break his ribs with his kick, but even without the broken bones, the resulting injury reminded Jack of the blow with every breath he took.

"You wouldn't happen to have a special pill in that bag that instantly heals me, would you?" Jack asked with a smile.

Casey snapped off her rubber gloves. "I'll have to ask the lab about that one. Last I heard it was still in production."

Chloe laughed from the backseat and Jack turned his smile on her. "So are you hanging in there, Miss Chloe?"

"Yeah, but I wish you hadn't gotten hurt again."

"You and me both. Don't worry, though. Your aunt is taking good care of me, and I'll mend eventually."

Casey stored all of the remaining supplies, then went into the store and returned with a Duke University baseball cap and a pair of sunglasses. She handed both to Jack, who donned them, then turned to Chloe.

"What do you think, Chloe? Am I stylin'?"

Chloe giggled. "Absolutely."

Casey started the car and Jack gave her directions to get to the freeway that would take them to Stevens's house. They had taken mostly back roads to get from the mountains to the highway ramp, but Jack figured the interstate was safer than trying to navigate the busy neighborhoods that surrounded their targeted housing development in downtown Charlotte. People on the interstate were in too much of a hurry to notice a specific car, but every subdivision had at least one nosy neighbor who was aware of every vehicle that drove by.

They drove for about half an hour in silence before Casey suddenly started trembling and her hands tightened on the wheel.

"There's a cop back there," she whispered. "He's coming closer."

Jack turned and looked for the car, seeing a highway patrol cruiser about three car lengths behind. "Just drive normally. If he recognized the car, he'd already have his lights on."

Casey paled and she looked at Jack, her eyes wide. "Can we outrun him?"

Jack winked at her. "In a Toyota Camry? It's a great car, but not built for racing. Please, just take a deep breath. We're going to be okay."

"Jack?" Chloe asked, her voice fearful. "What do we do if he stops us?"

"We'll all just act naturally as if we're going to a friend's house. Sometimes if they pull you over, it's just something simple like a broken taillight. If you start acting scared, he'll know something's up."

"He's coming closer!" Casey whispered frantically.

Jack put his hand on Casey's shoulder and gave her a gentle squeeze. "Take a deep breath. You're doing fine. He's just doing a normal patrol, okay? As long as you don't do anything to draw his attention, he'll just drive on by."

Jack was surprised by the irony of the situation. Here he was giving someone he thought might be a fugitive tips about how to stay unnoticed by the police. Even so, it was a special situation calling for unusual tactics. He needed to fly below the radar until he found a way to exonerate himself from this mess and get Stevens behind bars where he belonged.

A flashback of Jaime appeared in his mind's eye; he could see her driving their car and the two of them laughing and singing a song along with the radio. Her hair was blowing in the wind from the open window and her face was pink from a light sunburn that made her look radiant and healthy. She smiled at him. "Jack…"

"Jack?" The image disappeared as quickly as it had appeared and suddenly he realized Casey was staring at him with worry in her eyes as she looked between him and the road in front of them. "Are you okay?"

Jack drew his lips into a thin line. Being with Casey reminded him just how good life could be when sharing it with the right person. This wasn't the time or place for reminiscing or thinking about the future, however. He tried to push the feelings aside and turn his focus back to the problem at hand, but it was harder than he would've imagined. "Sure. Where's the cop now?"

"He just passed us. I thought I'd still hang back for a while, though, just in case."

"That's a good plan. Just keep your eyes open

and turn off on exit fifty-nine. It's only a few more miles." He pulled his hand back and stared at it for a moment, then leaned back against the car door, putting as much space as he could between himself and Casey.

This was wrong. He shouldn't be feeling anything for her, and it was wrong to let himself think, even for a moment, that their relationship could ever go anywhere from here. Hadn't he learned his lesson with Jaime? Love was a fallacy. As soon as someone gave their heart away, it was just a matter of time before it got broken.

The time passed quickly as they made their way to Stevens's house. He lived in a small residential neighborhood and even though he had only been there twice before, Jack had no trouble avoiding the major thoroughfares and directing Casey down the side roads to their destination. Once they arrived, they circled the block, then parked a few doors down. Casey cut the engine and turned to Jack.

"Now what?"

"Now I go inside and see if I can find that satchel."

"How are you going to get in?"

Jack shrugged. "I think the less you know, the better."

Casey looked around thoughtfully. "It's broad daylight. Are you sure no one is going to notice you go in there, especially if you force the door?"

"I don't have a lot of choice. Right now we know that Stevens is still at the national park and won't be here for a while. I might not get another chance to do this." He looked back at Chloe. "You two stay put. I'll be back just as soon as I can." He reached for the door handle, but Casey stopped him.

"You're weak, Jack, and you're injured. Let me go with you. If nothing else, it will look less suspicious if both of us go. A single man with a hat and glasses is bound to raise an eyebrow or two from the neighbors, don't you think?"

Jack considered her words. She was right of course, but breaking and entering was a crime. He was prepared to suffer the consequences of his actions, but he didn't want her implicated in anything illegal at his behest. "Look, I don't have a warrant to go in there, and you could get in trouble with the law if we get caught. I'm talking about jail time. It's better if you stay here with Chloe."

Casey looked like she was about to laugh, and her reaction surprised him. Why was she taking his warning so lightly? He watched her curiously as she turned to Chloe.

"Sweetheart, you stay here in the car, and stay down on the seat so no one can see you, okay?" Chloe nodded and Casey turned back to Jack. "She'll be fine. You need my help, Jack, so let's do this."

Jack looked into Casey's eyes and saw grit and determination there. She was going to help him because she refused to accept any other option. It was that simple. On some level he knew that he needed her help, but he was also feeling protective and didn't want her in any more danger because of him.

"Are you sure?"

"Absolutely."

The next thing he knew, she was out of the car, had circled it and was helping him get out. He felt her slip something in his hand, and when he looked up in surprise, she winked at him and showed him another set of the same items in her own hands. Latex gloves from her medical kit. Smart girl—she'd ensured they wouldn't leave fingerprints.

They walked briskly along the sidewalk toward the house. His limp was heavy but she held his arm as if they were a couple out for a stroll and he leaned into her strength as they made their way up the street. When they got to Stevens's house, they walked right up to the door as if they were paying a social call. Jack quickly tested the front door and the windows, but everything was locked. Jack and Casey glanced around the neighborhood, and seeing no one, went around the back, thankful for the overgrown plants and trees that gave them cover from prying eyes.

Jack looked carefully for any signs of a security system, and seeing none, examined the lock on the back door. Unfortunately he also didn't have any tools with him that would help him pick the lock. He tried the windows, but finding them secured as well he returned to the back door. It had several small glass panes, and Jack took off his shoe and used it to break one of them. Then he reached his hand in the door and unlocked the deadbolt and knob. Casey followed him in.

Once they were safely inside, they started a systematic search for the missing satchel. Jack had made sure to describe it to her as they'd walked toward the house. With their gloves donned, they started digging through Stevens's belongings. Jack left her in the living room to look while he went down the hall and into the bedrooms.

The master bedroom was a mess, with dirty laundry and old newspapers strewn around the room. On the upside, the sheer quantity of mess meant that Stevens wouldn't be able to tell exactly what they'd searched. On the downside, the whole search process was disgusting. A funky smell came out of the bathroom and Jack found a dead mouse in the mousetrap that had obviously been there awhile. It was probably responsible for the stench.

He rummaged through the drawers and end tables, then looked through the closet, but still didn't find his quarry. Next he examined the ceiling for loose tiles or other places that would offer a good hiding place. He even searched under the bed, but still he found nothing. He did the same thorough search in the two guest bedrooms, but there was no satchel to be found in either room. He came back out to find Casey, who had evidently finished her search of the living room and was now rummaging through the kitchen cabinets.

"Find anything?" Jack asked hopefully, but he could already tell the answer by her expression before she said a word.

"Nope. Sorry. I can report that this guy is a

total slob who rarely does dishes or cleans anything else in this place."

"I can report the same." He rubbed his eyes and leaned heavily against a chair. He was really hurting and his strength was nearly gone. What he needed was about six weeks off so he could properly recuperate. Unfortunately he wasn't going to get it.

Casey's expression turned worried. "Are you okay?"

"Just disappointed," Jack answered. He didn't want Casey to know the full extent of his injuries, but he doubted he could fool her in the long run. He opted for trying to focus on the task at hand. "I realized the odds of finding the satchel were low, but I was really hoping it was here somewhere." He sighed. "I'm not sure how I'm going to prove this case in court without some kind of evidence."

There was a stack of papers on the table in front of him and he turned his attention to them. There were several unopened collection notices, and Jack picked up a couple of bank statements that were mixed in amongst the chaos. He glanced up and down reports, shocked at what he was seeing. Brett Stevens was beyond broke. Jack shifted through some more of the papers. It also looked like Stevens's house was in foreclosure, and the bank was attaching a lien against the mountain property that his uncle had left him a few years ago.

"Are those important?"

"They don't prove the conspiracy, but they supply motive. Brett wasn't lying the first time he attacked me when he said he needed the money. He's dug himself into a giant hole financially, and it looks like he's about to lose everything."

A knock at the back door made them both jump. Their eyes instantly met and Jack moved defensively as quickly as possible to block Casey from whoever was at the door. He couldn't do much to protect her in his current physical condition, but he would give it his best shot. Casey grabbed Jack's arm as they watched the doorknob turn. A moment passed. Then another. Then they both breathed a sigh of relief as Chloe stepped through the door.

"Find anything?" she asked, her voice hopeful.

Jack's body relaxed and Casey stepped around Jack. "I thought you were going to wait in the car."

Chloe shrugged. "I was, but the guy who lives in the house next door just came home. I saw him look at our car kinda funny, and then he went inside. Maybe it was nothing, but I thought you needed to know to be careful when you came out in case he looks out his window."

Casey raised an eyebrow at Jack, then smiled at her niece. "You did the right thing, Chloe. We didn't find much and it's time to get out of here. That guy you saw could be calling the police right now."

Jack nodded, then led the way out the back door and carefully around the house to the front again, looking cautiously for anyone who might see them in the process and keeping a wary eye on the neighbor's house. He saw no one, but didn't want to take any chances. A few minutes later they were back in the car.

Jack glanced back at Chloe to see how she was handling the situation. The girl blew a big pink bubble with her gum and then giggled when it popped and stuck to her cheeks and nose. Jack was glad to see her acting like a normal kid instead of the frightened and timid child he usually saw. For some reason, ever since they had run from the cabin, she had started to open up around him, little by little. It was a welcome change.

He sank down in the seat, thankful for the chance to rest for a few minutes. The medicine took the edge off the pain, but nothing seemed to help him shake off the exhaustion that had settled over him. He was weak, both mentally and physically. He knew he was pushing himself too hard, but he really didn't have a choice. He glanced over at Casey, who had started the engine.

"Let's get out of here."

"Sounds good to me." She pulled away from the curb. "Where are we headed? The national park was my best idea, and you saw how well that turned out."

Jack ran his good hand through his hair, careful to avoid his wounds. He knew he had very few options. "Let's head for Concord. I know a small motel there on the edge of town that won't cost very much. It's no-frills, but clean enough. Will that work for you? You can have whatever money I have in my wallet to help pay for it."

Casey nodded. "That works. I've had my fill of excitement for quite a while. No frills sounds perfect."

Jack closed his eyes. What now? How was he going to prove his innocence? He was back to square one—his bullet in Denton's body and nothing but his word against Stevens's about how it had gotten there. With a few subpoenas he could prove that Stevens's financial problems gave him motive, but without more, it wasn't enough to even get an arrest warrant, especially with the D.A. aligned against him.

Jack had lost any evidence he might have had about the conspiracy, and he couldn't bank on Lennox and his friend coming up with anything new, much less anything decisive. A wave of frustration swept over him. Why wouldn't Casey testify?

He could arrest her and take her in as a material witness, but he knew down deep that that wasn't the way to handle this situation. Casey wasn't just leery of law enforcement officers, she was downright scared. There was definitely more to the story than she was willing to share, and he would just have to keep working on it. Somehow he was going to have to discover her secrets and convince her to help him. It was his only hope.

He looked over at her, and she turned and gave him a tentative smile that made his chest tighten. Her blue eyes were stressed but still the prettiest he had ever seen, and her lips curved slightly in a way that squeezed his heart.

No matter how hard he tried, he couldn't deny that he had feelings for Casey growing within him, but he still didn't want to act on them. Instead he pushed them down and buried them deeply inside. He didn't want to care about anyone else. He didn't want the pain of losing someone ever again. Besides, if Casey was running from the law as he suspected, any relationship would be doomed anyway. At some point he would have to arrest her, and she would end up hating him and regretting all that she had done to help him.

He looked at her again, noticing the smoothness of her skin and the way her dark brown hair beautifully framed her face. She really did look like a princess. And more than that, she had exactly the kind of warm, generous heart a princess should have. Whatever man won that heart would be a lucky guy.

But what if God was giving him a chance to be the one to win this lovely lady? What if he could help her with her problems like she had helped him? Wasn't anything possible with God? He shifted as his feelings warred within him. What if God had brought Casey into his life for a reason? What if?

# ELEVEN

The motel was no-frills, as promised, but it was cheap, clean and secluded. They were able to get two adjoining rooms, and after unpacking the few items they had salvaged from the national park, they made a quick lunch in Jack's room from some supplies they had purchased at a grocery store.

There was no kitchenette, but there was a microwave and a small refrigerator, which made life a little easier and saved Casey from making multiple trips to the ice machine. After eating, Chloe asked to go read in the adjoining room. Casey let her go but stayed back to clean up the lunch leftovers.

Jack seemed to be watching her every move, and after a few minutes she started to feel a sense of foreboding and apprehension at his scrutiny. She put a clip on the bag of tortilla chips and stowed the rest of deli meats and cheeses they had bought for the sandwiches. Finally she couldn't take it anymore. She pulled a chair up to the side of the bed where he was resting and looked him directly in the eye.

"Okay, Jack. I can tell you want to talk to me about something. What's on your mind?"

Jack ran his hand through his hair. "Casey, I need your help. There's no other way to say it."

A sliver of fear went down her spine, but she steeled herself. With his serious expression, this couldn't be good. "With what?"

"I need you to testify about everything you've witnessed that Stevens has done and said."

Casey stood immediately and headed for the door, but Jack's voice stopped her.

"Princess, please don't leave. I wouldn't ask if there was any other way I could prove this case, but I've run out of options. Stevens took my computer and the evidence from Denton's cabin, and the bottom line is that we're down to my word against his about what actually happened in the forest. Even if we get the proof that the cases were fixed and I can prove the conspiracy, I could still get convicted for Denton's murder. You're the only one who can testify about what really happened out there, and about how Stevens has chased us down and tried to finish the job at your cabin and at the national park. Your testimony would be vital. It would put Stevens in prison where he belongs."

Casey fisted her hands and slowly turned to face Jack. His face was determined, yet pleading at the same time. It melted her heart, but it didn't weaken her resolve. She had no choice in the matter. There was no way she could ever do what he was asking. If she testified, she would lose Chloe forever. And for what? Her testimony wouldn't help Jack. No jury would take the word of a kidnapper.

"Don't you think I want to help you? I wish I could, Jack. I really do. It's just not possible."

"Did you see what happened when I got shot?"

She looked away. "It doesn't matter."

"Of course it matters!" Jack said forcefully.

Casey shook her head. "It doesn't matter because I can't testify."

"Did you see what happened?" He waited a moment, then slowly pulled himself to the side of the bed and stood. "Casey, please. Answer me." He took a couple of steps toward her, but stopped a few feet away. "Look, I know you're scared, and I know you're running from something, but I can help you. Whatever you've done, whatever has happened…"

"It's not that simple, Jack."

"If you've broken the law, I can make sure you get a deal. The situation might not even be as bad as you think. If you tell me what's going on, we can work through it together. I promise I'm on your side, and I'll do everything I can to help you."

Casey's heart squeezed at his words, but he just didn't understand what he was asking of her. She let him see the tears in her eyes, but when he took another step toward her she took a step back and put up her hands. "I'm sorry, Jack. I just can't." She brushed the tears away and quickly escaped into her room.

Once inside, she leaned against the door, hoping that he wouldn't come after her and keep trying to convince her to testify. Chloe shouldn't have to hear or see that. She wanted to do the right thing, but the right thing for Jack was the wrong thing for Chloe. Slowly the minutes passed. When he didn't knock or try to come through the door, she breathed a sigh of relief. Her heart felt like it was being ripped in two.

*Dear God, I want to help him, but I can't sac-*

*rifice Chloe to save him. What should I do? Please, Lord, let there be another way for me to help him.*

"I've got good news and bad news," Ben Lennox stated in a matter-of-fact tone.

"Shoot," Jack answered, turning so he could see Casey and Chloe waiting for him in the car as he talked on the throwaway cell they had purchased. The three of them had been holed up in the motel for the past two days and it was good to finally be out in the fresh air, even though there was still a risk that someone might recognize them.

They hadn't wanted to be near the motel in case the cell-phone signal was tracked, so they had driven about forty-five minutes away to make the call just in case. They were all going a little stir crazy at the motel. Jack had spent the time alternating between sleeping, eating microwave meals and beating the socks off the two women in rummy and canasta.

Sedentary life was difficult for him since he was a man of action, but he had to admit that the rest had done him good. He still hurt in a myriad of places, but his overall energy level had improved, and at this point, any improvement was welcome.

"My contact was able to analyze the logs from the evidence room at the FBI building. Colby handled hundreds of cases each year, but my guy says he has definite proof that five of the cases were tampered with during the last year. He didn't go back further in the logs, but it's possible that he could discover even more cases if he changed the parameters of his search."

"That's great news," Jack said enthusiastically, as the first hope he'd felt in days surged within him. "What's the problem?"

"The problem is that when he found out Colby was the target and you were involved, he refused to investigate any further without specific authorization from the chief. I mean, he has a point. You are wanted for questioning in a murder investigation and Colby is a very powerful man who is still threatening to move forward with an indictment against you. That's not exactly a secret around the office and I don't blame him for not wanting to get stuck in the middle of the situation. Anyway, he won't even send over what he has because he doesn't want anything traced back to him without the right paperwork in place to authorize his investigation. He put his results on a flash drive but he says we have to come get it if we want it. He won't even email me the files because the email could be traced back to him and he's afraid he'll get fired."

Jack shifted. He couldn't fault the man for wanting to protect his job. Colby and Stevens were powerful adversaries. Still, this was unexpected, but not insurmountable. "Fine. I'll go get the flash drive so we can take a look. Tell me when and where."

"He's up in Richmond, Virginia. Look, Jack. I'd go myself if I could, but I think Stevens is getting suspicious of me. He's been following me around lately. He claims someone broke into his house and was going through his papers. He hasn't actually accused me of anything, but I don't want to lead him to the drive if it turns out to be the key to this whole case. It's just too dangerous."

"It's not a problem, Ben. I'll go. Where do I head after I get to Richmond?"

"My friend said he'll leave the flash drive in a manila envelope behind the counter at the coffee shop on Fifth and Trenton. I'll tell him to put your name on it so there won't be any mistakes."

"Once I get it, it will be time for me to go to the chief. He deserves a head's up as to what we've uncovered before that happens. You know that, right?"

"Yeah, I know," Ben answered. "I'm going to go to Mendoza today and tell him everything we have. It's going to start a fireball rushing through this office and eventually the media, but it has to be done."

Jack paused a moment. "Did my computer ever show up?"

"No, Jack. I'm sorry. My guess is that Stevens destroyed it."

A sudden wave of anxiety rushed through Jack as he glanced once again at Casey and Chloe. "Ah, Ben, were you able to find out anything about the woman named Casey that I asked you about?"

"I did a preliminary search, but she didn't pop up immediately on any of the usual databases. I could probably find her if I spent a little more time at it, but honestly, Jack, I just didn't have the time to go any further with it." He shuffled through some papers. "I'm sorry. I wish I had more news to report."

Jack shrugged and tried not to let his voice reveal his disappointment. He was becoming more and more anxious to know Casey's history, and his concern for her and Chloe both was growing on a daily basis. Somehow he would find a way to help them, of that he had no doubt, but he was restless and frustrated that he still didn't know what he was up against. A part of him also hoped that with the evidence on the drive, maybe he wouldn't need Casey's testimony after all.

Either way, he was now one step closer to proving the conspiracy, and he felt a wave of hope surge within him. "No worries, Ben. I appreciate everything that you're doing. Once we get the flash drive, we'll be in business." He paused. "I'll contact you again once I have the drive in hand." He hung up and headed back to the car, where he told Casey and Chloe about the phone call.

"So we're headed to Richmond?" Casey responded. "That's about a three-hour drive. Are you sure you're up for it?"

"Sure." He met her eyes. "Look, it could be dangerous. I don't know the man that left the flash drive, so I don't know if he can be trusted. This could be a trap and I don't want to put you in danger. Most of the FBI thinks I'm a murderer, so they won't go easy on me if they happen to catch me—or anyone connected with me. Plus Stevens still has the all-points bulletin out on your car. We could get stopped anywhere along the road and arrested."

Casey didn't miss a beat. "You need this drive to prove the conspiracy, right?"

"Yes."

"And you're injured and shouldn't be driving, right?"

He looked away for a moment, uncomfortable that she was pointing out his weakness and quite aware that she was correct in her assessment. Finally he met her eyes again. "Yes, but I'll do whatever I have to do to make this right."

Casey grinned. "And I'll help you as much as I can."

He smiled, then heard Chloe giggle in the backseat. Soon all three of them were laughing, without being quite sure why. Okay, so his princess wouldn't testify, but she was still taking quite a few chances on his behalf, and he could never forget that she had already saved his life on numerous occasions. "You're the best, Princess. Did I ever tell you that?"

"Once or twice," Casey joked. "Let's go to Richmond."

# TWELVE

A little over three hours later Casey pulled up near the Richmond coffee shop. Jack had Casey park a few blocks away so she and Chloe would be out of the line of fire in case something went wrong.

The travel had drained him, even though he had done little but sleep during the short trip. He was frustrated that his body wasn't improving faster, but he had to admit that he hadn't given himself much of a chance. Casey had been able to remove the stitches from everything but his side wound and his new head wound while they had been at the motel, but he still wore a sling and limped heavily, and his skin was still painted with bruises that were all changing colors in different stages of healing. Although Casey predicted a full recovery, he knew it would take several more weeks and some physical therapy before he was back to his normal self.

Injured and worn down, he had to ask himself if he was really ready for the battle that lay ahead of him. Even if he gathered the evidence without a hitch, there was still a long, hard road to follow to see Stevens and Colby charged and convicted of their crimes.

And that was only if everything went without a hitch.

He paused before getting out of the car as a myriad of emotions swarmed him. "Look, Casey, if anything goes wrong, drive away, do you hear me? No matter how badly you want to help, drive away and don't look back."

"Are you expecting trouble?" she asked, her brow furrowed.

"I don't know what to expect," he answered truthfully. "I trust Ben, but I don't know this man that he's been dealing with, and Colby has friends and a mighty long reach. I won't know if it's a trap until I get in there. All I'm saying is that I don't want you arrested as an accessory if things go south."

He reached out and cupped her face with his hands, enjoying the warmth of her skin. She was so beautiful! He hoped someday when this was all over and he was exonerated he could convince her to confide in him, but he also knew that realistically, he might never see her again. The idea disturbed him more than he wanted to admit and he already felt a tightening in his chest just at the thought.

"Thank you—for everything." He touched her lips with his thumb and caressed the soft skin. "Be safe, Princess." He kissed her gently on the mouth and was delighted when she kissed him back. He heard Chloe giggling from the backseat and he broke the kiss with a smile.

"Take care of your aunt, okay, Chloe?" She nodded at him with a suddenly serious expression and he reached back with his good hand and gently touched her face. He was surprised that she actually allowed the contact and didn't pull away. "You're a great kid, Chloe. You're smart and beautiful, and you're special in here." He pointed to her heart. "Don't ever forget that, okay?" He gave the child his best smile, then got out of the car and limped toward the coffee shop.

It was slow going, but a few minutes later Jack stepped inside. The pungent odor of roasting beans immediately assailed him. There were only a few patrons sitting at the tables, including a young woman and man sitting at the coffee bar. He chose a seat a few chairs away from the couple and ordered an espresso. He was actually looking forward to the drink. Casey apparently didn't like coffee, and since she had been doing the shopping he hadn't had a cup since before he was shot, despite his two-cup-a-day habit he'd nurtured since college. The bitter taste and a jolt of caffeine would definitely be welcome. The waiter brought him his drink and picked up the cash Jack laid on the bar.

"I think someone left an envelope for me."

The waiter raised an eyebrow. "That so? What's your name?"

"Jack. Jack Mitchell." He took a sip of his drink and smiled at the taste.

"Yeah, I got it. Hold on a sec and I'll get it for you."

The man returned and laid the envelope in front of him, just as he saw the young couple get up and move toward him out of the corner of his eye.

"Freeze, Mitchell." With a sudden movement the woman pulled out her service revolver and pointed it directly at him.

For a second Jack considered going for his weapon, but stopped when he noticed that the young man had also pulled out his gun and was aiming it at him from the other side. Were these agents friends of Stevens, or was it safe to give himself up to them? The young man seemed to sense Jack's hesitance and took a step forward. "The lady said freeze, Mitchell. I suggest you do what she says."

Suddenly two more agents rushed in the door, now all four of them pointing their weapons at his chest. He noticed their telltale earpieces and realized they had been staking out the restaurant, just waiting for him to say his name out loud so they could make the arrest. He kept an eye open for Stevens, silently hoping that his old partner wasn't a part of this. If Stevens were here, Jack was as good as dead.

If not, he might actually have a chance.

His eyes darted back and forth between the four agents and he nodded. Trap or not, there was nothing he could do against four of them, especially not in his injured state. He said a silent prayer, then slowly put down his coffee cup. "Okay," he said softly. He put his good hand up in a motion of surrender. "You win."

The young man stepped forward and roughly pushed Jack's face against the counter while the woman kept her gun trained on his chest. He grabbed Jack's good hand and stretched it across the linoleum, then frisked him and quickly confiscated the weapon hidden in the waistband of Jack's pants. The man's harsh treatment made a shiver of apprehension run up Jack's spine.

Had he done the wrong thing? Was it too late? Once again, he considered trying to fight back, but saw another two men enter the store and approach. There was no way he could win against six of them. On a good day he might have still tried, but not today with his current wounds. And really, what was the point? It was humiliating to get arrested when he had done nothing wrong, but it was also time for the running to be over and for Mendoza and Lennox to help him move forward with the case.

Hopefully these agents were just following orders and hadn't been told anything about the conspiracy or the reasons behind the arrest. He said another silent prayer that these men were working for the right side and weren't Stevens's and Colby's pawns.

"I need that envelope," he muttered as the young man cuffed him. "It's evidence in an important case."

"Don't worry. It's coming with us." He grinned, but it wasn't a friendly expression. "I'll keep the cuffs in the front for now because of your injuries, but if you give us any trouble, I'll cuff you behind your back. You got it?"

"Yeah, tough guy, I got it."

The kid narrowed his eyes, then grabbed the envelope, pocketed it and pulled Jack toward the door with the other agents following. He didn't recognize any of their faces and imagined that Lennox and Mendoza were the only ones who knew what was really going on. To these agents, he was just a rogue agent that was accused of murder. He was led out of the restaurant and to a nondescript four-door sedan parked nearby. They put him in the back seat with an agent on either side of him, then drove off, heading straight back to Charlotte.

Jack glanced around the street as they left, hoping for one last chance to see Casey, but if she was still anywhere nearby, he didn't catch a glimpse of her. An emptiness he didn't expect filled him and gripped his heart. He missed her already and they had only been apart for a few minutes. It was crazy! He tried to conjure up images of Jaime, but the only pictures that came to mind were of Casey leaning over him and reassuring him after he had been shot, her clear blue eyes warm and full of sunshine.

\* \* \*

Casey lowered the newspaper she was pretending to read and watched the car disappear down the street. She'd left Chloe in the car only long enough so she could check on Jack and see what happened at the restaurant. The sight of him being arrested was like a cold fist twisting in her stomach. She didn't know what his future held, but she knew that their connection was now irretrievably broken.

She tossed the newspaper in a nearby trash can and headed back to her car as a hollowness settled in her chest. She had fallen for Jack. Even though she knew a relationship had never been possible, she still felt the wound of loss deeply inside. She had wanted—no, needed—him to go back to his world and leave her in hers, but even so, a small part of her had held out hope that something about their situation would change and give her even slightly more time with him.

It was a silly thought, really, but she just couldn't help it. Jack had been honorable, and such a far cry from the usual men she had known that he had seemed like a breath of fresh air in her stale little world. Now she would probably never see him ever again.

She hadn't seen Stevens or his pal, so she

hoped Jack was safe, but either way, there was nothing she could do to help him since he was now surrounded by law enforcement personnel.

Would Jack be convicted of murder because she was refusing to testify? A heaviness swept over her and she twisted her hands, considering the possibilities. Would Jack divulge their relationship when he was being questioned? She could almost guarantee that he would, which would lead to a search for her records to see if she'd have any credibility as a witness.

Once he discovered her secret, any kind thoughts he'd had about her would quickly dissipate, of that she was sure. Everything was well and truly over between them now. She glanced around to make sure she wasn't being followed and quickened her step. It was time to disappear again, but this time she was doing it with a broken heart.

# THIRTEEN

Jack was really hurting. He had been sitting in the interrogation room for over an hour, and his pain medication had worn off a while ago. It was odd that no one had questioned him so far. He was beginning to worry that Stevens had played a role in his arrest, after all. If that was the case, the evidence he'd needed from the flash drive in the envelope had probably disappeared, along with any chance he'd had of proving Stevens's and Colby's guilt.

Suddenly the door opened and Chief José Mendoza entered the room, puffing on a cigar. The man was obviously angry, but Jack could see concern beneath the tough veneer. "You're causing me a lot of headaches, Mitchell." His voice was gruff as he looked Jack up and down. "I've seen you look better."

"I've been better, believe me."

The door opened again and Ben Lennox entered the room. He nodded at Jack and Jack felt a measure of tension ease as the other agent took a seat across from him. Mendoza was visibly brusque and forceful, but he didn't expect less from his boss, especially after he had been missing for so long without any communication whatsoever. With Lennox in the room, it signified that Mendoza was ready to listen, which was a very good sign.

"First of all, let me just tell you how disgusted I am that neither one of you bothered to include me in this investigation," Mendoza said, his voice filled with ire. "If Lennox hadn't finally come and told me that you were going to be in Richmond today and explained what's been going on, I might have just arrested the both of you and thrown away the key."

Jack put up his hands in a motion of surrender. "I'm sorry, Chief. It's my fault, not Ben's. I just didn't know who I could trust, and we wanted to come to you with proof, not conjectures. Colby is a very powerful man, so if this all fell apart, I didn't want anybody else's career to be destroyed but my own. Now with this data from the computer lab, though, we actually have something to give you that might prove my conspiracy theory."

"Well, just so you know, it cost me every favor I had to bring you in safely. The chief up in Virginia helped me get a protective custody order in place in record speed. Word has spread that you're wanted for murder, and Stevens or Colby might have connections up there that we don't even know about. Once they picked you up, I didn't want any of those Virginia boys roughing you up, or worse."

"I appreciate that, Chief. I really do."

"While you're feeling all appreciative, you should also know that I had Lennox tell his friend at the crime lab that I authorized the investigation into the evidence room logs. The paperwork has all been filled out and made into an official part of the investigation."

Mendoza leaned forward and Jack could almost swear that he saw steam coming out of the man's ears. When the chief spoke, his voice was barely above a whisper, but Jack had no doubt that his threat was real. "If either one of you ever do something like this again without keeping me in the loop, I'll take your badges. Do you understand?"

"Yes, Chief," the two men said in unison.

Mendoza looked from one to the other, then

leaned back and popped an antacid into his mouth.

"Start at the beginning, Mitchell, and tell me what's been going on."

Jack nodded, then took a deep breath. "Well, you already knew that Stevens and I were investigating some cases where the outcome changed because evidence disappeared, including the Simpson case where the crucial evidence mysteriously vanished right before the trial. I went up into the woods to investigate a lead regarding a P.I. named Milo Denton. I think Denton was doing some of the dirty work for the group and helping to destroy the evidence. Anyway, Denton owned a cabin up there and I was hoping to find something that implicated both him and his coconspirators.

"I found a laptop and some other documents, and the next thing I knew, some guys were firing on me. I realized they were Denton, another guy named Fletcher and Stevens himself. One of them hit me, and I got Denton, and then Stevens came out of the woods from a different angle. He looked me right in the eye, admitted his involvement because of some bad gambling debts, and then shot me two more times and left me for dead."

"I see you're all bandaged up," Mendoza said, biting into his cigar, "and I admit you look rough, but how'd you survive?"

Jack saw the skepticism in his eyes, and instinctively knew that what he was about to say wasn't going to help the situation very much. "A woman named Casey and her niece were staying in a nearby cabin in the woods. She heard the gunshots and came to investigate. After she found me, she took me to her cabin and stitched me up. Apparently she's had some medical training."

"Apparently," Mendoza agreed. "And why didn't she take you to a hospital?"

Jack shrugged. "Part of it was because I was too badly injured to be moved very far. But mostly it was because she's running from something in her past. I haven't figured out what yet. Also, she was smart enough to realize that I was in danger. She knew, like I did, that if Stevens was willing to shoot me and leave me for dead in the woods, he wouldn't think twice about trying to finish the job in a hospital where they would have very little security."

Mendoza crushed out his cigar in the ashtray. "And why didn't we hear from you until we had to pick you up in a coffee shop in Richmond? You could have called, Jack."

"My injuries kept me out of it for several days, and once I did start to feel better I didn't have access to a phone. The cabin we used is really remote—very patchy cell coverage to the point where Casey didn't bother having a phone. When I was well enough for her to drive me to a pay phone, I didn't know who I could trust. Stevens and Fletcher showed up at the cabin almost two weeks after I'd been shot and tried to kill both me and the lady, then Stevens tried a third time in the national forest." He looked Mendoza directly in the eye. "I knew you needed proof, so when I did finally make it to a phone, I called Lennox. Stevens took my computer and all the evidence I confiscated at Denton's place, but Lennox had an idea that might have salvaged the whole case."

Ben nodded and opened a file. He pulled out the flash drive that was inside and laid it on the table. "My contact at the forensics lab found proof that the evidence logs have been tampered with in at least five of Colby's cases over the past twelve months. He outlined that evidence on this flash drive. Now that we have the okay from you to continue with the official investigation, he'll probably find even more."

Mendoza seemed to be considering Ben's words. Finally he spoke, his voice gruff. "Bring me a laptop and let's see what you have."

About half an hour later the three of them had waded through all of the files and could plainly see the changes that had been made to the inventory logs. Apparently key evidence in the cases in question either got mishandled and damaged, mislabeled or was flat out missing from the inventory sheets.

According to another file, the common users that could have made the changes were narrowed down to one specific inventory clerk. Each case had gone to court, and each case had been dismissed with prejudice because of the evidence problems. Colby had also been the prosecuting attorney in each case. It wasn't enough to convict Colby by itself, but it was certainly a start and it substantiated Jack's claims.

Mendoza leaned back, his features clearly disgusted with the proof of the conspiracy that he saw laid out in front of him. "Okay. We're going to go forward with this investigation. I see an indictment for this clerk, but what I don't see is evidence that Colby conspired to help, or that anybody else was involved. That's going to take a little more work."

He paused. "Look, Mitchell. You're one of my best agents, and I'll tell you, even though the bullet that killed the man we found in your trunk came from your gun, the rest of the forensics are sketchy at best. I don't have the report in front of me, but from what I remember, it supports your story. Somebody put that body in your car after he was shot somewhere else, but right now I don't have any proof that implicates anyone in particular in this conspiracy, not even the dead man. You're telling me Stevens is dirty. It's not enough that I believe you. What I need here is proof that Stevens tried to kill you and is somehow involved in this. I need something besides just you telling me, because he's got a plausible answer for everything. I can't get the charges against you dropped without more, especially if Colby is in this like you say. What more have you got?"

Jack rubbed his chin. "When I was arrested I had a bullet in a little bag in my pocket. That's the slug that came out of my shoulder. If you have the lab take a look, you'll see that it came out of Stevens's gun."

Mendoza shook his head. "He claims you fired first and he was just defending himself. The bottom line is that it's his word against yours." He paused and leaned forward. "I'd like to know what that woman saw—the one who found you in the woods. She's been with you the past few days, right? Can she corroborate your story?"

Jack blew out a breath. "To be perfectly honest, I'm not sure what she saw when Stevens shot me. She was hesitant to volunteer any information whatsoever about that initial encounter. She can definitely testify about how Stevens tried to kill us at her cabin, and she also saw what Stevens did at the national park."

Jack went through the details about what had happened at Casey's cabin and the national forest. When Jack was finished, Mendoza shook his head.

"I want to buy your story, Jack. I really do. But you've got to see how Stevens can turn this whole thing around and say that he was justified in using force because you were resisting arrest for Denton's murder. I have zero evidence that implicates Stevens in the conspiracy ring, or in attacking you beyond the bounds of his job. We need that woman to tell us what she knows. Bring her in and let's ask her some questions. From what you're telling me, she's just the corroboration we need to issue an arrest warrant for Stevens."

Jack shook his head. "We're going to have a problem with that. I don't know what Casey's history is, but it's clear she distrusts law enforcement officers. She wouldn't even tell me her last name. I know she originally came from Florida, but that's about it. I have no idea where she is now, and I'm sure her plan is to live under the radar." He turned to Ben. "Did you find out anything more about her?"

Ben opened another file. "I did, Jack, but you're not going to like it."

Jack felt his heart squeeze and he tightened his fists. He knew she had been hiding a secret, but deep down he'd hoped that it was something simple like tax evasion. Still, though, with Chloe's fearful behavior, he'd always suspected that it was something much worse. He steeled himself, waiting to hear.

"Casey's full name is Casey Ann Johnson." He pulled out a picture and sent it across the table. Jack picked it up and instantly recognized the face smiling back at him. It was Casey in a cap and gown and it looked recent. "She graduated from medical school at Florida State University in June and had accepted a residency assignment at the Southeastern Regional Medical Center near Atlanta. However…" he paused for emphasis "…she never arrived in Atlanta because Casey Johnson is now wanted for kidnapping."

A knot twisted in Jack's gut. Kidnapping? Casey had kidnapped Chloe? The child had never been anything but loving toward her aunt, and Chloe sure didn't act like a kidnap victim.

"That doesn't make sense," Jack said, forcefully enough that Mendoza raised an eyebrow. "I saw how the two of them interacted. The child was scared of someone, but it sure wasn't Casey."

Mendoza shrugged. "We can get to the bottom of that later. For now, the conspiracy ring has to be our main focus. Kidnapper or not, you need to bring her in. We have a bunch of circumstantial evidence here against Stevens based on the story you're telling, but I gotta tell you, he's got a pretty condemning story against you, too, and like I said, right now it's boiling down to his word against yours. If we can't sort this out, at a minimum, you'll lose your badge. Worstcase scenario—you could end up convicted of murder."

Jack leaned back heavily, the weight of the situation pressing him down. How had things just escalated so quickly from bad to worse? He looked over at Lennox, who closed the file. "So where do we go from here?"

Mendoza stood. "I'll tell you what's going to happen." He pointed at Ben. "You're going to arrest that property clerk and officially open an investigation against Colby and Stevens. Lean on him hard and see if you can get him to talk. Find out if Stevens really does have gambling debts, and anything else you can come up with that supports Jack's story. Then get your buddy in Richmond on the case full-time to look into the rest of Colby's cases, but this time have him do it with the proper authorization. Tell him to focus on Denton, Stevens and Colby and anything they might have done on these cases. Let me know the second he finds anything new.

"Next, I want you to grab a forensic team and take them up to where Jack got shot and to this cabin where Jack claims Stevens tried to kill him. Have them reconstruct the scene if they can. Then give them this bullet Ms. Johnson took out of his shoulder and send it to the lab. And go over to the national park and question that park ranger." He paused. "You got all that?" When Ben nodded, Mendoza turned back to Jack. "Mitchell, you look like death warmed over."

"I'm ready for duty, Chief. I've got to find Casey before Stevens does. He already shot at her at the cabin. Once he figures out that this whole case hinges on her testimony, he'll stop at nothing to eliminate both her and the girl."

Mendoza shook his head. "Have you looked in a mirror lately?" He stood. "You're going to see a doctor, and then I've got to put you and Stevens both on administrative leave until we get this sorted out."

Jack was instantly incensed. "You're not going to take him into custody? He'll kill her, Chief." He surged to his feet, but staggered as the sudden movement caused his head to swim.

"Sit back down before you fall down," Mendoza ordered. Jack complied, frustrated, and Mendoza put his hand on Jack's good shoulder. "We can't take him into custody until we get evidence against him. Go to the doctor, but take Jorge Garcia along for the ride and tell him everything you know about Casey. He can start looking for your witness while the doc is giving you a thorough—and I mean thorough—exam. Then after the doctor is done, write out your statement and give it to Jorge. All I have right now is a bunch of circumstantial evidence, and I need proof!"

He paused and studied his agent. "I know you, Jack. I know that even on administrative leave, you're gonna try to work on this case, but I want you healed up, do you hear me? You're not going to do yourself or anyone else any good if you don't give yourself some time to heal." He waited for Jack to nod and then continued, "Get yourself a new computer and tablet and investigate with those. Work with Jorge and let him do the running around while you're healing up. Tell him everything. He's a good investigator and can do the legwork while you're down. I want that woman brought in, and I want to know everything that she saw out in the woods. Then I want her to tell me everything that happened when Stevens came back and tried to kill you. Kidnapper or not, if she backs up your story, we'll have enough to stop Stevens, and maybe we'll get lucky and even get him to flip on Colby."

He seemed to be considering something as he took a step toward the door, then turned back. "Jack, in an abundance of caution, I'd love to have Stevens charged and arrested, even though what we have is thin, but I'll tell you right now that it's going to be impossible to get Colby to request the arrest warrant from a judge. Even if I could somehow convince Colby that it's in his best interest to cooperate, if Stevens gets a decent attorney, he'll be out on the streets again in twenty-four hours anyway. The faster you find her, the better." He glared at the two men and lowered his voice to a menacing threat. "Don't forget what I said. If you ever even *think* of pulling something like this again, I'll take your badges. I mean it." He spun on his heel and left, leaving the door to close slowly behind him.

Jack stared at his computer screen at the arrest warrant that had been issued for Casey Johnson. He hit Print, then rubbed his hand over his eyes as he leaned back in his office chair. Everything was beginning to make sense now—the reason she wouldn't share her last name or say a word about her background. Even the fact that she had been able to save his life with her medical training made sense. The only thing that wasn't fully comprehensible was why somebody with her history would throw it all away to kidnap a little girl. Casey must have had a very good reason. She obviously loved Chloe, and Chloe had been jittery and fearful of men. Had someone hurt the child? Casey must have kidnapped the girl to protect her. It was the only thing that made sense, but so far, he had found no record to prove it.

He went back to his computer. How did Chloe's father figure into the picture? He was the one with legal custody. If Casey had taken Chloe away from him, she must have felt she truly had no other option. But why? What had happened? He still had dozens of questions, and there was only one way to find out. He was going to have to ask her face-to-face.

He stood and grabbed his jacket. If Mendoza caught him here at the office he'd be in trouble, but he'd had to get a few things from his desk before he headed for home. The doctor had checked him out and ordered six weeks of recuperation, which included some physical therapy for his leg and shoulder, but Jack just didn't have the time to lie around and wait for his body to heal.

He turned and caught sight of Stevens coming through the doorway across the room. In Jack's eyes, he didn't even look like the same partner he had known and worked with the past five years. Now he could see that bitterness had enveloped the man, and that he was clearly out to take what the world hadn't given him. Their eyes met across the room, and Stevens smiled at him, but it was a smile of pure maliciousness that promised retribution.

Jack turned away. How could he have ever called that man his friend? Why hadn't he seen the evil lurking beneath the surface? He knew that Stevens wouldn't stop until every loose end was tied up, which gave him precious little time to find Casey and Chloe.

He limped toward the door with his new tablet, leaving Stevens behind him. His physical condition notwithstanding, he had to find Casey, and he would not stop until he succeeded. He needed her—not just to exonerate himself, but also to make sure that Stevens remained behind bars where he couldn't hurt her or Chloe. He was also duty bound to execute the arrest warrant for kidnapping, and morally bound to investigate the circumstances surrounding it. Reluctant or not, Casey Johnson had just been bumped to the top of his witness list, and finding her and Chloe both had become his primary objective.

Jack turned in his statement and other paperwork to the appropriate staff, then caught Jorge Garcia's eye and motioned for him to follow him. The Charlotte FBI office had split their support nearly equally between Mitchell and Stevens; so much so that the animosity and distrust were thick and palpable throughout the room. Some offered encouragement and welcomed him back, but an equal number turned away as he walked through the room. Jack was both relieved and thankful that the chief had believed his story, and also pleased that his boss had given him Jorge to work with. The young man was a talented investigator, and hadn't been there long enough to become embroiled in the office politics yet.

"Where to, Jack?" Jorge asked.

Jack handed him a copy of his statement so he could read up on the case. He had already asked Jorge to do some background research for him while he'd been at the doctor's office.

"Let's go to Concord," Jack said quietly as they left the building and headed toward the parking garage. "I want to check out the motel and see if Casey is still there. I doubt she is, but even if she's not, maybe she left behind some clue that would tell us where she's heading."

"I'm supposed to be taking you home so you can rest." Jorge smiled. "I guess it's just going to take us a while to get there."

Jack nodded at him, glad that the younger agent understood that stopping the investigation wasn't an option, even with his poor health and leave status.

They got the car and headed to the motel where he and Casey had been staying. For the first half an hour of the trip, Jack told Jorge everything he knew about the case. Jorge asked several questions, and by the end of the conversation, Jack was satisfied that Jorge had enough to go on. The rest of the drive was completed mostly in silence.

Jack was actually glad for the reprieve and took the chance to rest. The doctor had given him medication that made him feel lightheaded. He hated the lack of clarity at a time when it was so essential that he think sharply, but he welcomed the relief from the pain. His body was still healing and wasn't shy about reminding him that he was still doing way too much too soon. Regardless of his aches and pains, however, Jack knew he had to find Casey and Chloe as fast as possible before they either disappeared again, or before Stevens found them first.

Casey's car wasn't parked at the hotel, and Jack hadn't seen it anywhere along the way as they'd driven along the road, even though he'd been keeping an eye open for it the entire route. The two men walked around the building once first, checking for anything unusual before entering, but saw nothing out of the ordinary. The desk clerk gave them the key, but once they went inside, they discovered that it was obviously abandoned.

Jack's heart sank as he walked around the room, looking for anything that might have been left behind to give him a clue as to their whereabouts. There was nothing. He started checking the drawers, then smiled as he withdrew a folded sheet of notebook paper from inside the Gideon Bible. He opened it and discovered one of Chloe's colored-pencil drawings. It was a picture of the first cabin they had stayed in; the place where they had brought Jack after he had been shot.

The child had done a good job of capturing the look of the cabin. It was colored brightly in cheerful shades with whimsical smoke coming out of the chimney. Underneath the picture she had drawn several hearts as if the cabin had brought her several happy memories. Jack took the picture and folded it carefully, then put it in his back pocket. At this point, it was all he had left of them.

# FOURTEEN

Jack heated up a bowl of chili and a slab of corn bread and ensconced himself in his bedroom. Mendoza had gotten hold of Jack's medical report and had threatened to arrest him again if he tried to set foot back in the office before he was healed, but for now, that was okay with Jack. He knew he could do many of the same things he could do at the office right from his new tablet with his remote connection to the FBI databases and his telephone.

He opened up his computer and a folder full of documents that the investigating officer had faxed him from the kidnapping case down in Florida. Jack had a mission, and that was to discover everything he possibly could about Casey Johnson and Chloe Peterson. With his FBI clearance he had been allowed to see all of the officer's notes and reports, as well as transcripts from the interviews, including those with Casey's friends from her medical school, one of her professors and Chloe's father.

He read deeper into the file and discovered that Chloe's mother, Courtney Peterson, was Casey's younger sister who had died under suspicious circumstances about six months ago, just as Casey had said. Courtney had twice tried to get a domestic violence injunction against her husband, Daniel Peterson, and both times, the restraining order had been denied by the court. She had then filed for divorce and accused Daniel of stalking her, but again, she'd gotten no help from law enforcement, despite noticeable bruising that the investigating officer had noted in his report. Daniel had even gone to her job and threatened his wife in front of her coworkers. Those coworkers had given their own statements to the police, which had also been ignored.

Two days later Courtney had been found dead with a bullet in her brain. Daniel had had a believable alibi, and the gun had never been found; however Jack noted that the time of death had been skewed due to the body being thrown into a canal. He flipped a page and discovered that Daniel also owned the same caliber gun, even though he'd claimed it had been stolen years before. It had never been found or tested. Jack raised an eyebrow. Why hadn't anyone noticed the domestic violence issues and the huge red flags? Why had the history of power and control been ignored?

He pulled out another report. Apparently Daniel Peterson had been awarded sole custody of Chloe, despite Casey's attempt to gain it in family court after her sister's death. Casey had accused Daniel of child abuse. However, there had been scant proof and Chloe hadn't testified.

Jack turned to the computer and started searching for any child abuse reports that might have been called in to the abuse hotline and investigated by a child protection investigator. He found two reports, both of which described bruises on Chloe. However, Daniel had apparently been able to give reasonable explanations for the child's injuries, and both investigations had been closed with no conclusions that the girl showed indicators of abuse.

Jack turned next to the kidnapping reports. Two days after Casey's graduation from medical school, she had apparently picked up the child from school and neither person had been seen or heard from since. Daniel Peterson had immediately filed a missing child report and the police had issued an arrest warrant. There had been absolutely no record of any sightings of the two since the kidnapping had occurred.

Jack got back online with his computer and started checking property records. He soon discovered that the cabin where they had been staying belonged to a family of another medical student who was in the same graduating class— probably one of Casey's friends. Jack looked up their contact information and dialed, but a short fifteen minutes later he was back where he had started. The student claimed that he hadn't seen or heard from Casey since graduation, but also said that a group of five or six of them had used the cabin on several occasions during med school, and Casey knew she was always welcome to stay there whenever she wanted.

Jack leaned back and closed his eyes, weariness consuming him. Again his body was telling him that he was doing too much too soon, and again he was trying to ignore it. He pushed the paperwork aside and ate his chili that had turned cold in the bowl. He still hadn't found out what he had been looking for the most, and that was clues about where Casey would try to run next. Did she have any family to turn to or any other friends that would help her out?

He tried to focus but found it impossible. A few moments later he was out, sleeping despite all of the questions that were floating around in his head.

Casey stopped at the stop sign and looked both ways. There was nobody coming from either direction and she took a moment to just catch her breath and think. After Jack's arrest, she and Chloe had only returned briefly to the motel where they had been staying to retrieve their belongings before bunking in a cheap motel in a small town north of Charlotte for a couple of days. Now she was in a quandary and couldn't decide where to go next. Should she leave North Carolina for good? What they needed was cheap housing in an obscure location. And since rent would have to come out of her small savings that would quickly dwindle to nothing, she would also need a job somewhere nearby. She was hesitant to enter the workforce because contact with people meant that many more chances she would have of being recognized and arrested—and that was only if she was lucky enough to find a job that would pay her under the table. Still, it had to be done sooner or later.

She looked over at Chloe, who was coloring

another picture in the front seat. Chloe had been the happiest she'd ever seen her at her friend's cabin in the North Carolina mountains. Casey wondered about the wisdom of returning there, but the more she thought about it, the more she liked the idea. By now the authorities must have searched it and moved on. Would they ever need to come back and search it again? She doubted it. Maybe that cabin was the perfect place to hide— almost like hiding in plain sight. And the price was right—it was rent free. That would keep her from having to get a job for a little while longer. Jack and the FBI would surely never think that she would return there, would they? She said a silent prayer and felt such a peace about the decision that she turned left, heading for the interstate and the cabin that would surely bring a smile to her niece's face.

About an hour later Casey pulled up behind the cabin and shut off the engine. Chloe had been so involved in her artwork that she hadn't even noticed where they had been heading, and now she slowly took in her surroundings, then looked at her aunt in surprise.

"What are we doing here?"

"Well," Casey answered, "I can't imagine why the police would need to come back here at this point. By now they've already investigated everything. Since this was such an excellent place to hide before, I thought we might as well come back." She touched the child tenderly on the cheek. "You liked it here, didn't you?"

The smile she got in response warmed Casey's heart. "Absolutely."

They got out and stretched, then walked up to the cabin. There was still crime tape crossing the door, but Casey pulled it off and unlocked the door before stepping gingerly inside. Stevens or law enforcement had obviously searched the place and left it a mess, but it wouldn't take much to fix it back up again. She owed it to the owners to leave it better than she found it anyway. She eyed the bullet holes in the wood, and memories of her time with Jack came flooding back—Jack smiling at her, Jack standing for the first time since his injury and taking a step. A wave of regret swept over her, but she pushed it aside. She didn't have time to think about dreams that would never happen. Jack was gone, and she would never lay eyes on him again.

She rolled up her sleeves. "Okay, kiddo, let's unpack the car and then get to work. You still have a little more math to do, too, and I want to make sure that assignment gets done before dinner."

Chloe made a face, but it was short-lived, and she skipped outside again and started picking up the wood that was scattered over the porch.

Casey watched her go, her heart full. She loved the little girl so much. She could never regret the sacrifices she had made for the child. If she was able to keep her safe, everything she had given up would be worth it.

A week later, Jack was feeling stronger, but was still no closer to discovering Casey's whereabouts. She had left no visible trail that he could find. She apparently was not close to her parents and hadn't had any contact with either one since her graduation. She had been very close to her sister, but it had been only the two siblings growing up and she didn't seem to have close relationships with any of her extended family, small that it was. She did have a small group of friends from medical school, but all claimed they that hadn't heard from her since graduation. In fact, no one would admit to seeing or talking to her since she had disappeared with Chloe.

On that fateful day she had withdrawn about fifteen thousand dollars in cash from her savings account, and hadn't touched any account since. She hadn't used a credit card from then on, either, or signed in to any of her internet accounts. For all intents and purposes, Casey Johnson had vanished.

Jack looked over at Chloe's drawing that he had put on his refrigerator door. He hadn't known Casey that long, but she had woven herself into his heart. How was he going to arrest her once he found her? She had saved his life—twice. She had nursed him and supported him as he'd struggled to prove his innocence. Putting handcuffs on her would definitely be the hardest thing he had ever been forced to do. And after he arrested her, how was he ever going to convince her to testify on his behalf against Stevens? She would hate him, and worst of all, Chloe would have to go back to her father. The more he looked into the situation, the more he was convinced that Peterson was a horrible person and probably guilty of his wife's murder.

He thought about Chloe and the fear that he had seen her display on a regular basis while he had been recuperating. The child had definitely seen some terrible things, or been victimized herself. He wasn't an expert, but her behavior definitely seemed to corroborate everything that he was reading. It was no wonder that Casey had felt forced to take Chloe away from the situation to save her from facing the same fate as the child's mother. Would he have behaved any differently if he'd had a niece or nephew in a similar situation? What was the right answer when the law failed you?

He looked back at the picture Chloe had drawn and just sat there looking at it, mesmerized by the colors and design as his mind wandered. Could Casey have gone back to the cabin? Under Ben's supervision, the FBI had sent the forensic team up on the same day that Jack had been arrested, and once they had finished gathering evidence from there and the place in the woods where he had been shot, there would be no reason for anyone from law enforcement to return. But would Casey think to return there?

Jack was out of leads. Even working with Jorge, who had brought fresh eyes to the case, he hadn't turned up anything new. He had already followed every other trail, so it was time to take a chance. If nothing else, he could look for more clues. Maybe he would see something that the others had missed, since he had actually known Casey for a few weeks and picked up on some of her mannerisms and lifestyle habits.

Jack stood and retrieved a soda from the refrigerator, then walked into his bedroom to get a jacket. As he did, he noticed the picture of Jaime sitting on his dresser. It was an outdoor shot with the sun shining on her hair and her sweetest smile lighting her eyes. He stopped and picked up the picture, studying it closely. The shot was taken before Jaime had known about the cancer, and he remembered that back then she had been full of life and brimming with plans for the future.

He ran his hands over the frame, lost in thought. He missed her so much, yet at the same time, knowing Casey had helped ease the pain in a way that he had never imagined.

What would Jaime have thought about Casey? He smiled, thinking that the two ladies would have probably been fast friends. They were both strong women with many admirable traits. His mind fast-forwarded to Jaime lying in bed, her body ravaged by cancer. She had told him to find someone new and encouraged him to live his life to the fullest, but until now, it had seemed impossible to even consider a new relationship with anyone else.

He sat slowly on the bed, the picture still in his hands. He had been angry at God when Jaime had died, but his anger had finally given way to thankfulness for the time they'd had together, however short it had been. Even so, the loss he had felt had nearly destroyed him, and he had decided never to fall in love again to protect his heart.

Had he been wrong?

He closed his eyes and bowed his head. *Lord, I'm not sure what You have in store for my future. This time next month I might even be in prison. I have strong feelings for Casey, Lord. I might even love her. Is it okay to move forward and love someone new? What if I fall in love with Casey and I lose her, too? I don't think I'm strong enough for that. Please help me know Your will for my life.*

He sat for another minute or so, a slow peace invading him, then opened his top drawer and placed the picture inside. He would always love Jaime, but his life with her was over, and it was time to move forward to whatever his future held. He didn't know when or if he would find Casey again, but he decided that if God granted him a second chance with her, he wasn't going to let her go. It was time to take a risk, and he knew that whatever happened, God would be there with him.

He stood and put on his jacket, then headed for his car. His arm was doing much better, but he still used the sling for the most part. Even so, he felt like he could take the sling off for the drive over and avoid taking Jorge with him. This was one investigation he wanted to do by himself.

# FIFTEEN

Casey snipped several green-headed coneflowers and put them in her basket, careful not to crush the other flowers she had already picked. Although several wildflowers bloomed in North Carolina in the fall, the coneflowers were probably her favorite. They reminded her of sunflowers, and the vibrant blooms always made her feel bright and sunny inside. She snipped a couple more, then moved toward another group of plants, enjoying the warmth of the sun on her face.

Casey had taken pleasure in being outdoors ever since she was a small child. She had many fond memories of bringing her parents wildflowers from the woods and her mother putting the blooms in makeshift vases all over the house. Now taking runs in the acres surrounding the cabin was one of her favorite activities, and she had discovered several different types of flowers that grew in the meadows nearby. She snipped a couple of light purple flowers, then stretched. She was actually starting to feel good about her decision to return to the cabin. Chloe had settled back into her school routine, and Casey was starting to relax and actually think about the future and where it would lead her. With each snip of the scissors, she felt more and more at peace.

"Hello, Princess."

Casey froze. Hearing Jack's voice brought a rush of emotions bubbling to the surface, but fear topped them all. Her heart started beating faster and she slowly turned her head toward the voice. Jack stood about ten feet away from her. He was dressed casually in khakis and a navy shirt, but she could tell that he had on his shoulder holster under his tweed jacket and his weapon was easily within reach. How had he gotten so close to her without her even realizing it? She hadn't heard a sound during his approach.

"I'd appreciate it if you'd put those scissors down," he said quietly.

She glanced up and met his eyes. He was here on business. She could see it in the way he was standing and the look on his face. All her hopes and dreams suddenly came crashing down around her, and her hands started shaking uncontrollably. He knew. She could see it in his eyes. He'd found out the details of her past and knew everything she had done. She felt a measure of relief that it was out in the open, but it was short-lived and quickly drowned out with dread.

"Do you think I'd stab you?"

Jack pursed his lips. "No, I sure hope not. But in my line of work, you can't be too careful. Sometimes people react in ways you'd never expect."

For some reason Casey couldn't identify, her grip on the scissors became tighter and tighter until her fingers started turning white. Her brain whirled, but she just couldn't figure any way out of this situation. Jack seemed to notice her distress and put up his hands in a peaceful gesture.

"Please, Casey. Just put the scissors down. I don't want anyone to get hurt."

For the life of her Casey couldn't figure out why she was hesitating. Even injured, she knew she could never defeat Jack and his gun with a pair of scissors, but for some reason, logic just wasn't fitting into the equation and she just couldn't let go. She felt frozen, like an ice sculpture. She couldn't even think of what her next move should be. A moment passed, then another.

Finally she found the words to express herself and respond.

"But someone will get hurt, Jack. If you arrest me, Chloe will have to go back and live with that monster. Her father killed her mother right in front of her. Did you know that? She can't go back there. If she does, he might kill her, too."

Jack raised an eyebrow. "I read the files, Casey. Her mother's death was suspicious, yes, but I never saw anything about Chloe witnessing the murder."

"She was too frightened to tell the authorities, but she told me. If you knew the history…" Her voice trailed off.

"I want to know. I want you to tell me. Give me the scissors, Casey," Jack said quietly. "I promise I will listen to everything you have to say and I will do all I can to help you and Chloe both." He took a step toward her, then another. "Please. You have my word on it. You saved my life, Casey. I won't forget that."

This time Jack's motion startled Casey and her paralysis finally broke. She took a step back, trying to maintain the distance between them. No matter what he said, she wasn't quite ready to give herself up. He stopped when she retreated, but his eyes were intense and seemed to bore right through her. She couldn't maintain the eye contact and looked away.

"There's no place for you to go, Princess."

"You're still injured," Casey said, her voice shaking as badly as her hands.

"That's true," Jack acknowledged. "But I had a great doctor. I'm feeling much better." He took another step, and once again she backed away from him. "Look, I'm not going to use my gun. I won't shoot you if you try to escape." He motioned with one of his hands, keeping the other up in front of him. "But you should know that my car is right around that bend. Even if you get away from me here, and that's a big if, I'll make it to the cabin and Chloe before you do." He took another step. "But that's not how I want this to happen." His voice was low and nonthreatening, and he moved slowly, trying to get her to look at him again. "I know you don't have any reason to trust me, but I'm asking you to anyway. I want to help, I really do, and I *will* help you. That's a promise. I want to do what is best for Chloe."

Casey finally looked up, her eyes filled with tears. "*I'm* what's best for Chloe. Do you think I would have given up everything if I could have found another way? Her father is a cold-blooded murderer. Domestic violence is his way of life. He terrorized my sister until he took her life. He'll do the same to Chloe if he's given the chance. I'm her only hope." She paused, her tone heavy. "Do you know how many abuse reports got called in on Daniel?"

Jack shook his head. "I read two. They were both closed with no indicators."

"That's right. It turns out the investigator they sent out was a friend of Daniel's, so the results of the investigations aren't really a surprise, are they? Daniel is a very popular man with a very long reach. He'd dynamic and charming. He's also the biggest manipulator I've ever met." She took a step back.

"My sister called the police seven times, Jack. Seven times! She got nowhere. Daniel was beating her on a regular basis, and no one would help. After the police would leave, the attacks would just get worse, so eventually she stopped calling. She tried to get an injunction for protection, but the judge wouldn't issue the order. After a while, Daniel figured out how to hurt her so the bruises wouldn't even show."

She choked on a sob, but continued, "Finally she decided she'd had enough and she decided to leave. She packed up Chloe and was heading out the door when he came home from work early and stopped her. He beat her in front of Chloe, and then pushed her down the stairs. She was hurt, but still alive, so Daniel dragged her and Chloe both outside and drove them away from the house. Then Daniel shot my sister right in front of his daughter and promised to do the same to Chloe if she ever told anyone what she had seen."

Jack was silent for a moment. His eyes showed empathy, but she could tell that he could not be swayed. "I do understand, Casey, and if I had been in your shoes, I might have even done the same thing. But is this the type of life you want Chloe to have? Living on the run? Never able to talk about her past? Constantly scared that someone will discover her true identity?" He took another step, and this time she didn't move away. "You both need closure after what happened in Florida, and if her father is the monster you say he is, he needs to pay for his crimes before he hurts someone else. Domestic violence won't just disappear."

He softened his voice. "We can work on this together. The law has failed you, but I won't. Please just hand me the scissors and don't fight me on this. I meant it when I said I didn't want anyone to get hurt."

Jack moved again and stopped right in front of her, mere inches away. He was so close that she could see the dark flecks in his brown eyes and smell the mint on his breath. Her heart was beating like a bass drum and it was all she could do not to throw herself into his arms and beg for his help. She knew she would still end up in jail, but maybe, just maybe, he was true to his word and would use whatever clout FBI agents had to make sure Chloe was safe. She knew she didn't have a lot of options.

Could she trust him? Did she have a choice? She wiped away tears and studied his face. There was compassion there but also unyielding strength, despite his physical condition. He didn't say another word, just put out his hand expectantly.

Casey took a deep breath, then turned the scissors so the handles were out and handed them to Jack. He gave her a tender smile, took the scissors and put them in his back pocket, at the same time removing a set of handcuffs. "Thank you, Casey. You did the right thing." He reached for her arms and snapped the sliver bracelets on her wrists, and she did not resist. "Casey Johnson, you're under arrest for kidnapping. You have the right to remain silent...."

He droned through the rest of the Miranda warnings but Casey barely heard him. What was to become of Chloe? What would her father do when he once again had the child under his control? She made a conscious effort to try to stop shaking as a wave of terror swept over her, but it was a losing battle. She'd hoped to never hear those words, especially from Jack, and now all of her worst fears were coming true. She had failed. Her sister had died, she had traded a promising career for a jail cell and now Chloe would be forced to live with her vicious monster of a father. Where was God? Why was he allowing this to happen?

"Do you understand these rights?"

Casey looked up again, jolted from her thoughts. It was all she could do not to weep uncontrollably. "Yes, I understand. What happens now?"

Jack reached down and retrieved her basket of flowers, then gently started guiding her to the road and his car. "Well, I'm not allowed to transport you back to town with Chloe in the same car since Chloe is officially considered the victim, so I called for backup. Someone should be here relatively soon. In the meantime, I thought I'd let you explain what's happening to Chloe so she won't be so scared." He paused. "You'll have a chance to say goodbye."

"These handcuffs will scare her."

"I imagine you're right, but I can't help it. Some things have to be done by the book."

Casey stumbled and Jack instantly grabbed her arm, supporting her. His touch gave her comfort, but only for a moment. She was sure their friendship had burnt to a cinder when he had realized she was a fugitive. Surely FBI agents would avoid any kind of relationship with kidnappers. The thought slashed even more pain through her heart, even though deep down she'd already realized that there was no chance for the attraction and love she was feeling to ever mature into any kind of long-term relationship.

She glanced up at Jack as they walked. His face was unreadable, but she had to admit, she probably would have been treated much worse if anyone else had arrested her. Despite everything he must have read about her that had been splashed in the files, he was still willing to give her a chance to see Chloe and explain what was happening so the little girl wouldn't be traumatized even further. She was thankful for that.

Jack was a good man, and he obviously did his job well, with dedication and consideration for those around him. Despite the fact that he was arresting her, her admiration for him went up a notch. If the law enforcement personnel down in Florida had been half as dedicated in searching for the truth, she would never have had to run in the first place and Chloe's father would already be in prison where he belonged.

Jack couldn't seem to let go of Casey's arm. Arresting her had been the hardest thing he'd ever done, and he was still struggling with his decision. Yes, what she had done had been wrong, but under the same circumstances, he wasn't sure that he wouldn't have done the exact same thing. What was that old adage, "There but by the grace of God go I"?

Even though Casey had committed a crime, he'd seen enough cases go sour to know that what should happen didn't always work out for the best, and that sometimes, justice didn't always occur in the end. That was reality; the legal system was far from perfect. He understood why she had kidnapped the child and didn't think less of her for desperately doing anything she could to save her niece before it was too late.

He worried about Chloe and where she would end up once the dust settled. Unfortunately the child-welfare system was just as imperfect as the legal system. He'd meant it, though, when he'd said he would do all he could to help make sure Chloe was safe. If what Casey had said about Chloe's father was true, there had to be some way of keeping the child away from the man. Jack had a few favors to call in, and he was already planning who he was going to phone and what he was going to say as soon as he got back to the office.

They turned the bend and his car came into view, but Jack was instantly alert the second he noticed another car parked behind his.

"That's far enough, Mitchell."

Jack looked for the voice and saw Stevens emerge from the woods, his pistol pointed at Casey. Jack pushed her behind him, shielding her with his body as Stevens approached.

"How'd you find me up here?" Jack asked, playing for time. He'd seen that look in his partner's eyes before. It was the same look he'd seen right before Stevens had shot him the last time.

"Tracking devices—standard FBI issue. One on your car and one in your favorite jacket." He smiled, but it was an evil smile. "Thanks for leading me right to our witness."

Stevens was only a few feet away now, and

Jack charged him, going for the gun. A shot rang out as they struggled, but it went wild. Finally the gun went flying, but Stevens was quick and hit him hard on his injured shoulder, then kicked him viciously on his leg wound. Both blows exploded with pain and Jack fell to his knees, struggling to recover.

When Stevens approached him again, Jack still couldn't stand, so he reeled against him, tackling him to the ground in a football-style move. On most days Jack could have taken Stevens, but not today, with his injuries only partially healed. The two men rolled, struggling for supremacy, but Stevens pelted Jack's shoulder again and again until he emerged on top with Jack pinned beneath him. He raised his fist and slammed Jack in the nose. Blood spurted everywhere.

"That's for humiliating me in front of every single person I work with." He hit him again, and Jack could feel his nose breaking as blood poured down his face. "Why couldn't you just leave things alone? You had to be the hero, had to get in the way."

"Stop!" Casey yelled, drawing both men's attention. She had picked up Stevens's weapon and was pointing it at him, her hands still cuffed and visibly shaking. Jack was instantly glad that he had cuffed her in front instead of the normal procedure of cuffing suspects with the hands behind their backs. A whisper of hope surged within him.

"You don't want to shoot an FBI agent, lady. You're in enough trouble already."

"You would know, Agent Stevens, wouldn't you? Looks to me like you'll be getting your own cell just down the hall from mine."

"I'm not going to jail," Stevens said defiantly. With a quickness Jack had never seen before, Stevens pulled a second gun out of his ankle holster at the same time that he pulled Jack up as a shield in front of him. "Put the gun down right now, lady, or I'll shoot the both of you right here on the road."

Casey's hands trembled even harder and Jack could see the indecision in her eyes. His brain was foggy from pain and he was physically exhausted, yet he still searched for some way to help her. He made one last move to knock the gun out of Stevens's hands, but the move was anticipated, blocked and followed by a hard blow on his side wound. Jack flinched and groaned as Stevens put the barrel of the gun against Jack's temple.

"I said put the gun down—or I'm going to blow this man's brains all over the ground."

"Don't do it, Casey," Jack said, his voice rough. "After he shoots me, you shoot him. You can do it. Just aim and pull the trigger."

"Shut up," Stevens barked, hitting Jack against the head with the gun. The blow caused bright flashes of light before his eyes and he struggled to stay conscious. "I'll give you to the count of three, lady, and then I'm killing him, and then you. Got it? One…two…"

"Don't!" Casey dropped the gun and stepped back, her eyes filled with tears.

Stevens nodded and viciously pushed Jack face down to the ground. After grabbing Jack's gun, he went over and retrieved the gun Casey had dropped as she rushed to Jack's side. She helped roll him over, then cupped his face in her hands.

"Oh, Jack, can you hear me?" Bits of dirt and debris had become embedded in his cheeks and forehead and she used her sleeve to wipe the blood and rubble away.

Jack could feel her hands checking his injuries and warmth spread through him. Her touch was comforting, even though he realized somewhere in the back of his mind that he probably didn't have much longer to live.

"Thanks, Princess. You're always saving me." His voice came out raggedly, but she smiled at him and gingerly traced his eyebrows with her fingers.

"I love you, Jack. Didn't you know that? I couldn't watch him kill you." Her voice was soft and for his ears alone.

What? Had he just heard her correctly? She loved him? His heart swelled and despite his surprise he could see the light in her eyes that testified to the truth of her words. "You'll always be my princess."

"Get up," Stevens ordered as he nudged Casey with the gun. "Put Jack into the back of my car."

Casey gave Stevens a look of surprise and he repeated himself, motioning with the weapon. "Get him up and over to the car. Now."

Casey bent over and helped Jack to a sitting position, then somehow managed to give him enough support for him to make it to his feet. "You'd think I'd be used to carrying you by now," she quipped, her voice laced with nervousness as she worked to overcome the fear.

Jack struggled to move even with her ministrations, but gave a small smile at her effort to distract him. "Yeah, seems like we've done this before a time or two."

"Shut up," Stevens ordered. He walked over to the car and opened the back door, then put one of his guns back in his ankle holster while he kept the other trained on his two victims. Once he had them both in the backseat, he threw a set of cuffs at Casey. "Here. Put these on Mitchell."

She did as he ordered and Stevens checked them, then shut the door and got behind the wheel. He started the motor and headed down the road.

Jack could barely keep himself upright, and after a few minutes, he lost the battle and sank down against Casey, who shifted and helped him lie down with his head against her leg. Her hands were still cuffed, but she gently touched his face and ran her hands through his hair, being careful of his injuries. It felt wonderful. Her touch was light and sent soothing tingles through his skin, distracting him from the pain in his nose and shoulder.

The drive was short and after only about twenty minutes, Stevens pulled off the main street and headed down a small dirt side road. The car jolted over the bumps on the poorly maintained road, and each one sent even more waves of agony through Jack as he struggled to stay conscious. Finally he gave up the battle and passed out completely. The last thing he remembered was seeing Casey's beautiful blue eyes looking down at him, filled with love.

# SIXTEEN

Jack awoke later and found himself lying on a dirty wooden floor in a very dark room. The smell of mold and decay permeated his senses. The lone window was apparently boarded up, but a thin sliver of light fell between two of the boards and offered him a scant look of the space around him. Bits of dust floated in the light, and when he moved slightly a plume of dust billowed around him.

"Hello? Anyone here?" he asked softly.

"Jack?" Casey appeared from the darkness. "I'm so glad you're awake!" She knelt next to him and touched his arm gently.

"You wouldn't happen to have any aspirin in your pocket, would you?" Jack asked quietly. His entire body seemed to be pounding with pain.

"Nope, sorry. I don't usually take medicine out with me when I go flower picking."

Jack moaned as he shifted. "I think Stevens succeeded in breaking whatever wasn't hurting before today."

"You are officially my most persistent patient," Casey said softly, and he could hear the smile in her voice. "As soon as I try to get you healed up from one encounter, you find Stevens another time and manage to get stomped into the ground all over again."

Jack laughed. "Well, that wasn't the plan, I assure you." He tried to get a good view of his princess but there just wasn't enough light. "It's amazing you haven't given up on me. You haven't exactly seen me at my best. You must think I'm a total failure as a law enforcement officer."

"Why? Because you can't stop a bullet with your bare hands? Because you can't heal yourself overnight? When you do learn those tricks, let me know. You'll be a medical marvel and I'll be your press agent. We'll make millions selling your story to the tabloids."

"Deal," he said with a smile, then groaned as he moved again and felt the pain radiate in his shoulder. The throbbing sobered him and he tried to wipe some of the blood out of his eyes. "Look, I'm sorry, Casey. You wouldn't be here now if I hadn't led him right to you."

"You didn't know he was tracking you and I'm sure this afternoon didn't turn out how you'd planned, either." He heard her stand. "Right now let's just figure out how to get out of here. I hate to sound like a broken record, but you really need to get to a hospital."

Jack thought a minute, even though his head still felt fuzzy and he found it hard to focus. He tried to remember if he'd had anything in his pockets when he arrested Casey that could help them now. He could tell that Stevens had taken his weapon. "Casey, can you reach into my jacket pocket? I had the handcuff keys in there, unless Stevens took them." He shifted uncomfortably. Apparently Stevens had also left the scissors in his back pocket, but he didn't mention them quite yet.

Casey crouched down again, reached into his pocket and felt around for the key. A few seconds later she withdrew her hand victoriously. "This is great! I can't believe he didn't check you better."

"Well, he's not really at the top of his game. He used to be a good cop, if you can believe it. Now I don't even recognize him."

She didn't comment as she undid his cuffs, then handed him the key. He undid hers and put both sets in his pocket. After the cuffs were gone, she rubbed her wrists and leaned back on her heels. "I'm so worried about Chloe. We've been in here for over an hour and Stevens still hasn't returned."

She paused. "I don't think you heard him because you were pretty out of it, but Stevens said he was going to go get Chloe and come back and kill us all. I'm not in a hurry to die or anything, but I'm really scared for her."

"Don't worry. My guess is that he's in custody and Chloe is fine." He coughed, and pain swept through his chest. The sound of it must have scared Casey because she leaned closer and started carefully touching his side where Stevens had brutally pounded his fists against his wounds.

"Does this hurt?" She moved her hands and he gasped, then groaned. "I think you've got a couple of broken ribs in there." She touched his face, gaining his attention. "I know it hurts to cough, but coughing actually helps. It prevents secretions from pooling in the lungs, which could cause pneumonia." She felt for his pulse and watched the rise and fall of his chest. "You're not coughing up blood and your heart rate and breathing seem normal. Those are all good signs."

"Thanks, doc."

"So what makes you think Stevens is in custody and Chloe is okay?"

Jack coughed again and grimaced. "Well, like I told you before, once I knew for sure that you were back at the cabin, I called in for backup. They were supposed to meet me there to give Chloe a ride down so I could take you in." He tried to move his arm and groaned. He wasn't a doctor, but he guessed that Stevens had also dislocated his shoulder.

"If Stevens had to take the time to grab us and bring us back here before heading to the cabin, then there's no way he could have gotten to Chloe before the backup arrived. He has no legitimate reason to be there, and my blood on his clothes will make it pretty clear he was in a fight. I highly doubt they'll let him just walk away. They've probably already arrested him. That's the explanation that makes the most sense for why he's not here. Stevens definitely wanted both of us dead, and he doesn't make idle threats. If he could have gotten back to hurt us already, he would have."

"Why didn't he just kill us before instead of stashing us in here?"

"My guess is that he has to make it look like

an accident. He's already being investigated for shooting me the first time. Now the FBI is watching him and he can't afford to make any more mistakes. He was probably planning to get Chloe and then make it look like the three of us died together in some freak car accident that he devised."

Casey stood up, disgusted. "I can't believe he still hasn't been arrested after everything he did."

Jack coughed again. "The problem was that most of the evidence against him was circumstantial—or a case of his word against mine. He said I was the one who tried to kill him, not the other way around."

"That's crazy."

Jack tried to catch her eye, but with such low light it was all but impossible. He could almost guarantee that Casey had seen more that she had admitted, but could he convince her to talk about it? She was already under arrest, so did she still think she needed to hide the truth from him? That was the question. "Well, there're only a few people that really know what happened out there," he hedged.

He eyed her intensely, trying to read her expression before finally deciding to go with the blunt approach. "Princess, did you actually see me get shot? Did you see everything that happened?"

Casey got quiet and looked away, but Jack pushed forward. "After we're found, I really need you to tell your side of the story. Your testimony will make all the difference. If you describe everything you saw, Stevens will go to prison for a long time."

Casey stood up quickly and moved away from him. He caught a glimpse of the distress on her face, but he didn't understand. Why was she still refusing to testify? Did she continue to think there was some way to escape? Was she going to leave him here and try to make it out on her own so she could disappear without going to jail?

He had to admit, if she tried to get away without him, there was very little he could do about it. He was in no physical shape to stop her. But the mere idea of her leaving him behind ripped his heart in two. It had very little to do with how it would hurt his case.

If Casey ran, the law would come down even harder on her when they caught her again. And they would find her. Casey was no professional, and eventually she would make a mistake. Jack could guarantee it. No, what she needed was to stay and face the consequences of the kidnapping charge. Only then could she put it behind her.

A fugitive's existence was filled with constant fear and stress. It ruined lives. He didn't want that for her. He didn't want her to waste her talent that way and throw away the wonderful gift of healing that God had given her. Casey was an amazing doctor, and Jack was sure that God had a marvelous plan for her. He was even starting to hope that that plan might somehow include him. Could he convince her that their future was worth fighting for?

He tried to push himself up with his good arm, holding his injured arm close to his chest. He felt beads of sweat pop out on his forehead from the effort, but he finally made it to a sitting position.

He looked around and tried to get his bearings. The room was small and seemed like some sort of storage shed. He saw several cardboard boxes in the immediate vicinity, but little else.

"Casey?"

She reappeared but didn't come very close. Her face was definitely hard to read in the dim light.

"Princess, what are you thinking?"

She didn't answer so he tried to stand. As he was struggling, she came over and helped him, her arms warm and soft. After she got him up, she moved her hands along his shoulder and felt that the arm bone was strangely positioned in front of the joint. He cringed at her touch and she could feel the muscle spasm under her fingers.

"Jack, you've dislocated your shoulder." She moved his arm slightly and he groaned in pain.

"I was afraid of that."

She met his eyes. "I know you don't want to hear this, but we need to put it back in, and it's going to hurt when I do. Let's get you in a sitting position."

She helped him sit back down and lean against the wall. With gentle hands she flexed the elbow to a ninety-degree angle and gradually rotated the shoulder outward. He groaned loudly and a few minutes later, she felt the bone slide back into place. Despite the cold, Jack was sweating and his muscles were trembling from the injury.

"We need to put that arm in a sling. Are you wearing a T-shirt under there?" When he nodded she continued, "Good. I'll help you take it off and we can use that. I'll tear it into strips and knot it together."

She moved to help him take off his jacket but he stopped her and touched her cheek softly. He saw a single tear run slowly down her face and he caught it with his finger, then pulled her as close as he could in a warm embrace with his good arm. "Casey, what's wrong?"

She didn't answer for a few moments, but finally blew out a breath. He felt her stiffen as she pushed forward, her voice a mere whisper. "I tried it your way, Jack. I tried to get help for my sister from the cops down in Florida, but they wouldn't believe anything that I said. They didn't believe me after she was dead, either, and they refused to investigate. The law doesn't work for me, Jack, so you see, it really doesn't matter what I saw or didn't see out in the woods that day, or what I've witnessed Stevens do since that first attack.

"But even if by some strange quirk of fate it did matter, nobody is going to be interested in anything I have to say now anyway. I'm a kidnapper. I freely admit that I took Chloe away from her father. I did it because I was afraid he would kill her and I honestly didn't know what else to do. My testimony would only hurt you."

She stopped on a sob and Jack pulled her closer. "I'm so sorry, Casey. I can't make you any promises about how it's all going to turn out. Our system isn't perfect, and sometimes it doesn't work the way it should. But I do know this. I'm going to do everything I can to help you and Chloe. I believe you, and I'm on your side."

She took a moment to respond, and when she did, her voice was shaky. "I'm just so scared, Jack. Everything is happening so fast. I knew some day this could all catch up to me, but I just wasn't ready for it to happen today. Maybe I never would have been ready. I just don't know." She gave a weak smile. "Have you ever made plans for your life and then had everything go terribly, terribly wrong?"

Jack touched her cheek tenderly. "Actually, I have. I was married, like I told you, and we planned a future full of picket fences and the American dream. Cancer got Jaime after we'd been married about two years."

Casey's face fell and she bit her bottom lip. "Jack, I'm so sorry. Here I am acting like Chloe and I are the only ones that have ever suffered in this life. That must have been horrible to see someone you loved going through something so devastating."

"Well, I didn't have to watch her suffer through an abusive relationship, like you did with your sister, but it was horrible in its own way. I've spent quite a bit of time learning to live with it and accepting God's plan for my life. But through all of that, I never thought I'd have those types of feelings for someone ever again. Now, though, I'm not so sure."

With his good hand he reached down and took her hand, then brought it to his lips. "I've been fighting against my feelings for you because I didn't want to open myself up again to the hurt and pain that comes with losing someone you love." He kissed her fingers gently. "But it's been a losing battle." He touched her chin and lifted her face so he could see her eyes. "I love you, Casey Johnson." He moved his mouth to hers and kissed her, and it was filled with promise.

"Casey, please don't try to do this on your own. Let's do this together. I know you're scared, and I also know that once we get out of here, you'll be tempted to disappear and try to help Chloe on your own. I know my limitations, Casey. I won't be able to stop you." He leaned closer, his lips near her ear. "But please don't try it," he whispered. "Don't do it." Her eyes got wide as if he was reading her thoughts and he pushed forward. "Trust me. Let me help you. Let the law work for you."

"It never has before."

"It can now. I'm on your side. I won't let you down." Jack was scared, too, because if Casey escaped him and tried to kidnap Chloe again, she would be taking her chances against Daniel Peterson, Chloe's father.

If Peterson was capable of murdering his wife in front of his child, then he was apparently capable of anything—including vengeance. Hunting his sister-in-law down to make her pay for taking Chloe would be child's play. "Casey, I'm weak right now. I know it and you know it. I can't force you to stay. I'm not physically strong enough to do it, but even if I could, that's not how I would want it to go down, anyway. I'm not even sure how we're going to get out of here yet, but I do know this. If you run, I'll find you, and then it will be even harder to prove your allegations against Peterson."

He felt her stiffen in his arms. "Is that a threat?"

"No, Casey. I'm just telling you how it is. But I won't find you because you broke the law. I'll find you because I love you, and I don't want you to throw your life away like this. You're a talented doctor who has a lot to give. I've been amazed since I met you, Princess. You've stuck by me through thick and thin and saved my life over and over again. Now it's my turn. Let me help you. Let me show you how the law is supposed to work."

He squeezed her fingers gently. "I need you, too, Casey. I need you to testify against Stevens and verify my story. We can help each other. Casey, will you save my life again? Will you testify to help me clear my name and put Stevens in prison?"

"Is that was this is all about? You need me to testify?"

"No. This is about trust and love. Neither one will disappear if you refuse."

Casey's heart was beating so fast she was sure it was going to come right out of her chest. He loved her? Was this for real, or was he just saying the words because he wanted her help with his case?

She looked into his eyes, and even in the dim light she was able to see the truth mirrored back at her. He loved her, even if she chose to never testify. But could she do it? Could she let him take her to prison, and face the courts for her crime? Because of his injuries, all she had to do was find a way out of the building and she would be free. She could hike back into civilization and disappear. Chloe would be shipped back to her father, but if Casey was patient, Daniel would eventually let his guard down and she could kidnap Chloe again.

Instead of leaving the state, this time, they could leave the country. It wasn't a perfect solution, but if she got arrested now, she'd be stuck in a jail cell. She could do nothing to help Chloe from there. Could she allow herself to be detained and give up the chance to get Chloe away from Daniel one last time?

Jack was right about one thing. He was weak, and in his injured state, there was no way he could physically force her to stay. In fact, he probably would need to depend upon her just to get out of this shack and back to civilization alive. Escape from him would be easy, and was just about guaranteed. So why was she hesitating?

"Let's get this jacket off you and take care of that sling for your arm," she said quietly. "Then we'll check the building and see if there's a way out of here."

Jack was obviously hoping for a different answer, but he let her change the subject without argument. Their discussion had already probably worn him out. Carefully they removed his jacket and shirt, then she pulled off his T-shirt and tore it into strips to wrap around his chest to bind his ribs, and to fashion a crude sling for his arm.

"I'm sorry we don't have a better way to do this," she said softly. She could see the paleness of his skin and knew the pain had to be excruciating. "Look, Jack, you'd better lie back before you fall down."

He nodded his agreement, and once they had his shirt and jacket back on, she gingerly helped him sit and then stretch out on the floor.

"I'm trying to find a way out of this building, but there is only one door and it's locked from the outside."

"Your scissors are in my back pocket," he whispered. "You can break the windows and then maybe use them to pry the boards off. It's worth a shot."

She leaned over and retrieved her scissors, then bent and gave him a quick kiss on the lips. "Thanks. That's a good idea." His lips were soft and she lingered for a moment, then returned to the task at hand. She didn't want to make any big decisions right now; she just wanted to get out of this building and get help for Jack. There would be time later to figure out what her next move should be.

There were a couple of boxes in front of the

window, and she moved them out of the way before stepping up to the panes. She turned the handles of the scissors toward the glass and hit it hard, then stepped back as the glass shattered and cold air rushed inside.

"Are you okay?" Jack asked, trying to push himself up again.

"Shh. I'm fine. Lie back down and let me work on this for a minute or two." He did what she asked, but she could tell that it was hard on him not to be helping with their escape. She decided to tell him what she was doing so he would feel more involved. "It looks like there're just two boards over the window, and each board is attached in three places, top, middle and bottom." She broke the rough edges of the remaining glass away from the frame and groaned as she tried to pry the nails out with the tips of the scissors. They wouldn't budge. "These nails are in here too tightly to get out with the scissors. I'm going to feel around the room to see if I can find something else to use, like a hammer."

"If you help me up, I'll help you look." Jack suggested, his voice again telling her that he was straining to stand back up.

"Jack Mitchell, would you please listen to your doctor? Stay lying down and rest, okay? As soon as we get out of here, we have a long hike in front of us. I would appreciate it if you would rest now so you'll be ready."

Jack laughed, but ended up coughing. Still, when he spoke, there was mirth in his voice. "Whatever you say, Princess."

She found a shelf with small boxes of nails and a big can of nuts and bolts, but no hammer or other tool. She felt spiderwebs and some sort of bug that scurried away from her, and a bin filled with items that felt like old car parts. She kept feeling around and came across some sort of canvas bag. It stunk of old sweat and mold, but inside she found a baseball bat and several old baseballs. It wasn't perfect, but it would do. She was no Babe Ruth, but it was worth a shot to see if she could break through the half-inch plywood that covered the window. She made her way back, aimed for the wood and took a swing.

"Whoa, what was that?"

Casey examined where she had hit the wood. It had come loose in the middle, but was still in place. "A baseball bat. Good thing I played in Little League. I always wondered if those skills would come in handy someday." She took another few swings and was finally rewarded with light shining into the window as one of the boards gave way. A few strikes later and the other board fell away, as well.

Casey looked over at Jack and her heart twisted. His face was still a bloody mess from where Stevens had beaten him, and his body language testified to his anguish. Still, the love for him that she was feeling swelled within her. She didn't want to leave him. Didn't want to run away again. But could she trust him? And even if he did everything he could, would it be enough? Would Chloe be safe?

She swallowed hard and just stood there for a moment, sorting through her options. What should she do?

Another thought hit her. What about Jack? He needed her to testify to support his story and save his career. Would he be able to prove his innocence without her, or would he be convicted of murder? Could she live with herself if Jack lost his job and went to prison when she could have prevented it? But what if Daniel Peterson hurt Chloe and she could have prevented that by kidnapping her once again and hiding the little girl away?

She closed her eyes and threw her head back,

searching for answers. Finally she did what she should have done from the beginning. She started to pray.

# SEVENTEEN

It had been tricky to get out of the window, but after putting cardboard over the fragments of glass to protect herself and throwing the bat outside in case she needed it, she had been able to shimmy through the small opening and get free of the building. Casey brushed herself off, then grabbed the bat and went for the door. There was a bolt by the handle, but no lock, and it was no trick at all to slide the metal bolt back from the casing and get the door open. Once inside again, she rushed to Jack's side. He had dozed off, but came to when she gently touched his face.

"Jack? Wake up, Jack. We're ready to blow this Popsicle stand and get out of here. Are you with me?" He moaned in response and she checked his breathing and heartbeat again. She knew a minute of fear when his pulse seemed thready, but readjusting her fingers gave her a better read and she breathed out in relief when she felt the stronger beat.

"Jack?"

"I'm with you, Princess. I just need a minute to regroup." He paused as if gathering his strength. "Can you help me stand up again?"

She helped him roll onto his good side, then put her shoulder under his good arm and gently helped him back to his feet. "Are you sure you're up for this hike, Jack? I could go by myself and send help."

"And then what?"

"What do you mean?"

Jack touched her cheek and brought her eyes to meet his. "Will you turn yourself in?"

She tried to look away but he wouldn't let her. He cupped her face with his hand and gently brushed his thumb against her lips as if willing her to speak. When she didn't answer his question, he finally sighed and withdrew his hand. "I'm ready to go whenever you are."

They made it out the door and started down the road, but it was a slow, painful process. Jack was limping and leaning heavily on Casey, but she found that she was enjoying the contact. Her time with Jack would soon be over, no matter what she decided. Despite the circumstances, she wanted to make the most of every moment they had left. But even as she nestled closer to him, her thoughts churned in her head with each step, no matter how hard she tried to keep them out.

After about thirty minutes, Jack stumbled and Casey had a very hard time getting him back to his feet. "Let's rest a few minutes," she suggested. Jack nodded, and she led him over to a nearby stand of trees, then helped him gingerly sink to the ground.

"I'm sorry I'm so much trouble," Jack said quietly. "This wasn't how I planned to spend the afternoon."

"Me, either," Casey replied with a smile, considering the irony, "but all things being equal, I'm glad that Stevens didn't find his way back to us." She squeezed his arm. "And you're not too much trouble. I think you're doing amazingly well, considering everything you've been through the past few weeks. It's impressive that you can stand at all. You should be in a hospital, and by the way, that's exactly where you're going once we reach civilization again. You know, Jell-O, ugly hospital gowns, the whole enchilada."

"I'm not sure what my future holds, but that description doesn't encourage me." He grimaced as he moved his back, apparently trying to find a more comfortable place to rest.

Casey felt the tone of the conversation change and a sense of dread swept over her. She wanted to encourage him, but she wasn't ready to give him the promise he wanted, either. She settled for giving him the answer to the question he'd been asking since they first met.

"I saw the shooting," she revealed, and then instantly regretted it. He raised an eyebrow but didn't comment, and she felt compelled to continue and fill the ensuing silence. Now that she'd admitted that much, she might as well tell him everything. "When I heard the first shots, I went to the edge of the cliff and could see everything that happened down below." She stopped, then continued, her voice soft. "At first I thought maybe it had something to do with Chloe and me and that you'd found our hiding place, but then I saw Stevens shoot you in cold blood. I was really scared when I went down to help you, but I just couldn't leave you there to die, no matter what it cost me."

Jack reached over and grasped her hand. "Thank you. You saved me, Princess. No matter what happens next, I know I owe my life to you." He grimaced as he tried to move, but he slowly bent forward and placed a kiss on her lips, then drew his fingers down her cheek.

Suddenly they heard a car engine, and they both turned their attention to the road. At first all they could see was a dust cloud, but then a black Suburban pulled into view. "Let's get behind the tree just in case I'm wrong about Stevens," Jack said quickly. Casey nodded her agreement, and she helped him up and into hiding.

Her heart pounded in fear until it felt like it would come right out of her chest as the vehicle came nearer. What if it was Stevens? What if he had returned with Chloe to kill the three of them? There was no way to outrun him, especially if he had his gun. If Stevens was the driver, it would only be a matter of time before he discovered that they had escaped and he would track them down again. She grasped Jack's good hand and held on tightly as the car approached.

Jack watched as the SUV made its way up the road, keeping his eyes on the driver. When the Suburban got within thirty feet or so, he breathed a sigh of relief and came out from behind the tree, motioning with his good hand. It was Ben Lennox. He said a silent prayer of thanks and then turned to Casey. Her face had suddenly turned pale and she was trembling. He grasped her hand again.

"It's okay, Casey. It's Ben Lennox, an agent from the FBI that I know and trust. Everything is going to be fine. This must mean that what I guessed was true. They have Stevens in custody and Chloe is safe. They probably offered him some sort of deal if he revealed where he was holding us."

Casey tried to take a step back, but Jack wouldn't release her hand. "Please, Casey. Don't run. Trust me."

Casey shook her head, her eyes wide, then turned her attention back to the vehicle that had stopped. A tall man in an FBI jacket nodded at Jack and was heading toward them. His weapon was clearly visible in a holster strapped to his hip. Jack nodded back, then locked eyes with Casey. "Please."

Jack's heart clenched as a single tear ran down Casey's cheek, but she finally nodded, then made a motion of futility with her hand and put her wrists together, ready for the cuffs. Jack pulled the silver bracelets out of his pocket and cuffed her, then turned to Ben.

"Jack, you're looking rough."

He smiled wryly. "I've been better."

"You look like you can barely stand up."

"That's pretty much accurate." He motioned to Casey. "This is Casey Johnson. She saved my life—yet again."

"I'm glad to hear that, but she's still wanted for kidnapping, isn't that right?"

"That's right, but she's also my witness. She saw everything Stevens did and can corroborate my story. Please treat her with kid gloves, okay?"

Ben rubbed his chin. "Whatever you say, Jack."

Jack swayed a little and Ben reached out to help him. "Let's get you to the car before you fall down."

Jack accepted his help and Casey stayed by his side. "Tell me what happened with Stevens."

Lennox glanced at Casey, then shrugged. "He's on the run. We figure he must have come up to the cabin to try to abduct the girl, but when he saw us waiting, he turned tail and ran. We got worried when you didn't show up and we found your car abandoned, so we've been searching for the both of you ever since. I was afraid Stevens might have tried to shoot you again." He handed Jack a handkerchief, and Jack wiped at the blood on his face as Ben continued, "Is he the one who did this to you?"

"Yeah," Jack admitted. "Right after I arrested Casey, Stevens appeared and took us by gunpoint. He locked us in a shed a little farther up the road. Casey was able to get out a window and open the door from the outside. We started walking and here we are." He looked up and down the road. "How'd you manage to find us?"

Lennox grinned. "I found out that Stevens's uncle left him some property down this road, so I took a chance. There's apparently a house and a few outbuildings." He opened the door to the SUV. "It's good to see you're still alive. I was wondering."

"Thanks. So where's Chloe?"

"She's safe and in custody with the local social services department. Her father has been notified."

"She can't go to her father's custody, Lennox. He's a murderer and killed his wife right in front of her. She'll be in danger if she goes home with him."

Ben raised an eyebrow. "Do you have proof? I never saw that in the file."

"If we handle it right and don't spook her, Chloe will probably testify. At a minimum we need to get a psychological evaluation done. Just keep her away from her father until we can get the investigation going, okay? As a favor to me?"

Ben laughed. "I'll add it to the list."

Jack stumbled and Ben and Casey both quickly helped him get back to his feet, gingerly avoiding aggravating his injuries. "We're taking you straight to the hospital as soon as I get this radioed in, but this time we're strapping you down so you don't get back up again until you let your body heal," Ben said grimly.

Together they managed to get Jack into the backseat of the Suburban so he could lie down. Casey tried to join him, but Ben objected and motioned toward the front seat. When he reached for her, Casey took a step back.

"Ms. Johnson, I've read your sheet. Are you going to start giving me trouble?"

Casey shook her head. "No, but I just graduated from medical school. I'm not an official doctor yet because I haven't completed my residency, but I want to keep an eye on his condition."

"It's okay," Jack offered. "I trust her."

Ben shrugged. "Your call, Jack." He moved out of the way so Casey could get in, then shut the door behind her.

Jack put his head on Casey's leg like a pillow and looked up into her eyes. "Have faith, Casey.

Everything will be fine. God has His hand on this."

Casey's chin trembled, but she nodded silently. Jack wanted to reassure her some more, but the pain was too great and he faded back into darkness once again.

# EIGHTEEN

*Six weeks later*

Jack drew his gun and motioned to Ben, who stood on the other side of the hotel room doorframe.

Ben knocked and disguised his voice. "Hotel manager, sir. We've had a noise complaint."

They heard footsteps inside, but they weren't coming toward them. Jack motioned to one of the other agents who was holding the battering ram and stepped aside so the man could reach the door. With a loud crack the ram smashed into the wood and the door opened as the frame splintered. The other agent stepped back and Jack and Ben rushed inside, guns drawn.

"FBI, Brett," Jack called out as they started their search. "We've got the hotel surrounded. You're not getting out of here. Give yourself up before someone gets hurt."

Ben headed for the bathroom, and a few seconds later he called out that the room was clear. Jack closed the closet and hurried to the sliding glass door and the balcony. Stevens's room was on the fifth floor of the hotel and the balcony was the only possible escape. Jack stepped outside and swept the area, looking for his quarry. He saw movement out of the corner of his eye and caught of glimpse of Stevens's feet disappearing above him into the balcony on his right.

It had been six weeks since Casey's arrest and Jack had healed considerably, but even if he'd been at death's door, there was no way he was letting Brett Stevens escape. Ben appeared beside him and could instantly see what was going on.

"Let me climb after him. You can go up to the sixth floor and get him if he doesn't keep climbing."

Jack shook his head, then put his foot up on the metal railing and hoisted himself up. It shimmied a little but supported his weight. "Nope. Brett Stevens is mine. Take the team and follow us up." From the new vantage point, he could see that Stevens had already swung up to the balcony on the next floor and was pulling himself up by the wrought-iron posts.

"He's still going up," Jack called to Ben as he

jumped to reach the next balcony. He gripped the railing and quickly dragged himself up by the balustrade, then swung over and landed on the balcony floor. His muscles were straining with the exertion, but he was determined to arrest Stevens. He mustered his strength and jumped to follow his prey. He reached the floor of the balcony that Stevens had just vacated and took a moment to catch his breath.

The bullet Stevens fired at him barely missed his head and shattered the tile about three inches from his nose. Jack rolled quickly and scrambled to his feet, then threw himself against the wall out of view as Stevens fired again and bits of stucco exploded around him.

Jack pulled his gun and quickly took a look to see if he could see get a glimpse of Stevens, but Stevens had already holstered his weapon and started climbing again. Jack secured his gun and continued the pursuit. He jumped to reach the iron railing of the next balcony, but his foot slipped and for a moment he hung only by his grip on the black metal rail, precariously dangling seven stories above the ground. His adrenalin surged and he was immediately grateful for all of the pull-ups he'd been forced to do in physical therapy after his shoulder injury.

He grunted and hauled himself up, ignoring the quiver of strain he felt in his shoulder. A few minutes later Jack reached the balcony of the highest floor and surveyed the area around him. He saw no access to the roof, and no sign of Stevens. Drawing his weapon once again, he stood against the wall and gingerly pushed at the sliding glass door. A quick look around proved that Stevens had vacated the room, and Jack exited to the hallway just in time to see the door to the stairwell swinging closed.

Jack lifted his wrist and spoke into his radio transmitter. "Stevens is on the stairs—west side of the building. I think he's going to the roof."

"Copy that," Ben answered. "We're on our way."

Jack advanced cautiously but quickly down the empty hallway and looked down the stairwell. He couldn't see anyone going down and there were no telltale sounds of anyone using the stairs, so he turned and headed up toward the rooftop that was only one flight away.

He opened the door and glanced outside with his weapon drawn, using the apartment wall as a shield. To his left he could just make out Stevens running away from him and he followed, using as much of the building as he could to protect himself in case Stevens decided to turn and fire. He took cover behind an air-conditioning unit just as more of Stevens's bullets smashed into the brick by his shoulder. He returned fire and ducked as Stevens fired three more times, each bullet ripping into the soft metal of the air conditioner.

"You're either leaving here in handcuffs or a body bag, Brett," Jack yelled out. "There's no other option." He did some quick math in his head. So far Stevens had fired ten shots. If he'd started with a full magazine, the standard issue FBI Glock 22 pistol held fifteen bullets. What Jack didn't know was whether or not Stevens still had his second pistol in his ankle holster.

He picked up some gravel from the roofing material and threw it to his right, and Stevens reacted quickly, firing three more times at the sound.

"The building is surrounded, Brett. It's only a matter of minutes before the team gets up here. I've already radioed in your position. Give yourself up now before we add any more charges to the list."

At first, silence met Jack's words, but finally, Stevens answered. "What's the difference? Either way, if I let you take me in, I'm headed for prison."

Jack crawled to his left and managed to make it behind a different AC unit right before another one of Stevens's bullets ricocheted off the fan only a few feet in front of him. He turned and fired at Stevens's position from the new angle and Stevens drilled another bullet into the brick behind him in return.

That was fifteen shots. It was time for a gamble. Stevens was desperate and stressed. He doubted the man had counted his bullets. Jack stood, his arms up in a motion of surrender.

"Prison's better than the needle," Jack contended. "Testify against Colby and you'll get a good deal."

Stevens rose slowly at the sight of Jack standing with his hands up. He advanced cautiously and stopped about five feet in front of him, his Glock still pointed at Jack's midriff. "You never were very smart," Stevens said with a smirk. He fired, and a look of shock crossed his face when the trigger just clicked in his hand.

"Rookie mistake, partner," Jack said softly.

Stevens's face instantly turned red with fury and he threw the gun to the side and tackled Jack, grabbing for Jack's gun. The two men struggled for supremacy and took several steps back as their feet slid along the gravel. A few seconds later they were at the edge of the building's rooftop and Stevens was pushing Jack against the edge of the wall. The waist-high barrier was the only thing keeping them from falling to the ground—nine stories below.

Jack still had a grip on his gun, but Stevens was holding his wrists so tightly that there was no way to get off a shot.

"I hope you can fly, Jack. You should have quit while you were ahead."

"I never quit," Jack gritted out. "And you are under arrest." It took every ounce of strength he had in him, but he slowly struggled back up so he was no longer leaning over the edge of the rooftop wall. He pulled and strained against Stevens's grip and pushed the other man back, first one step and then another. The second he was able to he brought his knee up hard into Stevens's leg, and his former partner groaned and loosened his grip on Jack's arms. It was just enough for Jack to be able to pull his wrists away and bring his gun hand over to knock Stevens on the side of the head with the butt of the weapon.

He staggered, but didn't go down. Instead he tried to throw a punch at Jack's stomach, but Jack anticipated the move and blocked it swiftly, then followed with his own punch to the chin and an uppercut to the gut.

Stevens fell back, blood dripping from his bottom lip, and Jack pointed his gun right at his former partner's head. "Now show me your ankle holster, slowly."

Stevens narrowed his eyes. "You won't shoot me. You've never been about revenge."

"True enough," Jack answered. "But tracking you down has never been about revenge. This is all about protecting the people I care about, and I'm not playing games. That means I will definitely shoot you if you try anything."

"We were partners for five years. Five years! Doesn't that count for something?"

"I offered to help you before, Brett, if you'll remember. Your response was shooting me four times and framing me for murder." Jack shook his head. "The weapon, Brett. Now. Pull it out slowly and only use two fingers. Got it?"

Stevens reached down and pulled up his pant leg, revealing the small pistol in the ankle holster. He pulled out the gun with two fingers as ordered and held it out. Jack took it and secured it in his waistband, but kept his own pistol trained on Stevens the entire time. "On your knees, hands on your head."

Stevens grimaced, but he did as he was told. His anger and frustration were evident with every move he made.

Jack pulled out his handcuffs and quickly secured Stevens's hands behind him, then patted him down to make sure there were no other weapons hidden on his body.

"How did you find me, Jack? I thought I did a pretty good job of making myself disappear."

Satisfied that Stevens was no longer a threat, he left him on his knees with his hands cuffed behind him and took a step back. Although he was feeling much better and had healed considerably from his injuries, he still wasn't 100 percent and the chase had taken a lot out of him.

"The Ford case. I remember we seized a stack of fake passports. I went back to the evidence locker and did a search to see if any were missing. When I found that one had disappeared, I assumed you had it and started searching for the name. It was just a matter of time before I got a hit and tracked you down."

Jack holstered his gun. "You must have stolen it a while ago, because it wasn't long before I discovered you already had a full identity with credit cards and bank accounts set up under the phony name, and none of them were new. I imagine we'll find what we need to corroborate my theory back in your hotel room."

Disgust painted Stevens's face. "That case was over three years ago. I can't believe you thought to go back and check that."

Jack shrugged, then leaned forward and pulled Stevens to his feet. "Let's just say I was extremely motivated to stop you before you hurt anybody else."

Suddenly the rooftop door slammed open and Ben and the rest of the FBI team entered, guns drawn. When they saw that Stevens was already secured, they relaxed their stance and lowered their weapons.

"Take him out of here," Jack said, motioning to his former partner. "It's over."

# NINETEEN

*Six months later*

"Okay, ladies and gentlemen. We're here today for a hearing on the department's motion for modification of placement for the minor child, Chloe Peterson, case number 11-403. Ms. Johnson, I understand that you are seeking custody of the child under the interstate compact and that she is your niece. Is that correct?"

Casey stood next to her attorney and addressed the judge. Her knees were knocking so loudly she was sure someone would comment. "Yes, Your Honor."

The judge turned to the attorney for the Department of Children and Families. "What does the department think?"

The attorney for the department stood. "We agree with the placement, Your Honor. As you know, the mother is deceased, and the father, Daniel Peterson, was recently convicted of murdering the child's mother. Now that the father's parental rights have been terminated, we want to establish permanency for this little girl. Ms. Johnson is the child's aunt, she has a positive home study and she is interested in adopting Chloe. We think that it is in the child's best interest to be placed with Ms. Johnson."

The judge flipped through the papers in the file and paused on one, taking a moment to read it. Finally he looked up, an expression of worry splashed across his elderly face. "And what about this kidnapping charge? It looks like there was a plea agreement put in place, but I'd still like to hear more about this."

The department's attorney didn't flinch. "Your Honor, Ms. Johnson did 'kidnap' the child under the letter of the law, but she was trying to protect Chloe Peterson from her father, a man that we now know brutally killed his wife in front of the child. I have Special Agent Jack Mitchell here from the FBI. He will gladly explain the situation and speak on Ms. Johnson's behalf."

"Good," the judge responded, looking over his glasses at Jack. "I'm very anxious to hear more about this. Proceed."

Jack approached the bench and was sworn in by the bailiff. Then, for the next fifteen minutes, he described how Casey had tried to use legal channels to protect the child, and when that had failed, how she had taken Chloe in order to keep her safe. He also delineated how she had saved his life and provided key testimony in the convictions of a rogue FBI agent and the district attorney in North Carolina, and how she had already served her time and had expressed remorse for her actions. The judge listened with rapt attention, then finally turned to Casey.

"Young lady, I don't condone breaking the law, but I understand your motives. You have served your time and done your utmost to take care of your niece. In light of the special agent's testimony, I see no reason why Chloe Peterson should not be placed with you. It is so ordered." He turned to the department's lawyer. "Next case, counselor."

"Is that it?" Casey whispered to her attorney.

"That's it," the attorney confirmed. "The department's case manager will bring Chloe by your hotel this afternoon. Then you're free to take her back to North Carolina. After she's lived with you for ninety days, we can file the petition for adoption." She closed her briefcase and led Casey out of the gallery to the hallway where Jack was waiting. The attorney shook Jack's hand and thanked him, then left, leaving the two of them alone in the hallway.

Casey gave him a huge smile and then a rambunctious hug. "Jack, you were magnificent! Can you believe it? It's all working out, just like you said!"

Jack laughed. "I'm just sorry you had to spend time in jail."

Casey sighed. The six months she had been incarcerated had been rough, but she couldn't say they had been all bad. Once he'd been released from the hospital, Jack had visited her every week on visiting day, and she had been able to start a bible study with three women in the jail who had committed their lives to Christ during their stay. She had even decided to go back once a month to encourage them with the bible study.

Jack grasped Casey's hand and led her down the hall and out to the courthouse steps. It was March and the Florida weather was sunny and mild. Large puffy clouds floated listlessly in the sky and gave Casey a peaceful feeling that she hadn't felt in months. The brilliance of the day made her think that her life was starting fresh this afternoon, once Chloe came home for good.

She turned to Jack, remembering the last

time they'd gone through a trial together. Testifying against Stevens had been one of the hardest things she had ever done, especially because the man had glared at her the entire time she had been on the witness stand. She had felt his hatred radiating at her throughout the testimony, yet because of her, Stevens had finally buckled and decided to take a plea, accepting a lesser prison term in exchange for testimony against Colby. Now both men were serving time in prison.

Jack had been totally exonerated and had healed completely from his wounds after a brief stay in the hospital and several weeks of physical therapy.

"It's beautiful out here, you know that?"

"You're beautiful," Jack answered, and leaned in for a kiss. His lips were soft and warm and Casey relished the way they felt against hers. Jack had fulfilled every one of his promises he'd made that day she had been arrested, and although she had been terrified of what lay before her, he had stood by her side through every step of the process.

He had made sure that the child abuse case against Daniel Peterson was reopened and that Chloe had been placed with an excellent foster family instead of with her father while the case was reinvestigated. With the FBI involved and a prominent child therapist who had stepped in at Jack's request to help Chloe with her trauma, they had also been able to find enough evidence to charge Peterson with murder.

With the therapist's aid and support from Casey and Jack, Chloe had found the strength to testify about the night Peterson had killed her mother, as well as to the other past instances of abuse. Her testimony had sealed the man's fate. Daniel Peterson was also behind bars tonight and would never hurt anyone again.

"God has blessed us in so many ways, Jack. It's overwhelming."

"Yes, He has." Jack pulled out an envelope from his coat pocket. "Are you ready for one more surprise?"

Casey caught her breath and smiled. "I don't know if I can take any more good news. I'm already so happy I could burst."

Jack returned the smile. "Sorry, but you have no choice. This is from the North Carolina Regional Research Hospital."

Casey covered her eyes. "I can't open it. Can you read it to me?" She peeked through her fingers at him as he ripped open the envelope. "'This letter is to inform you that you have been accepted for the residency program in the cancer wing...."' He didn't get any further before Casey squealed in delight and started dancing right there on the courthouse steps.

"Oh, Jack, I can't believe it! Thank you!" Casey still had to complete her residency before receiving her medical license, yet she had been turned down twice at other hospitals due to the kidnapping charge. This hospital had also voiced some concern about her crime, but Jack's unit chief had called in a favor and explained the entire situation to the chief of staff of the hospital. Because of his help, Casey's future in medicine was now guaranteed.

"God is so good, Jack. He's taken care of everything." She kissed him and smiled, truly content.

"He always does," Jack agreed. "Although not always in the way we expect." He paused, then met her eyes. There was a strange look in his, as if he was actually nervous about something. "I've got one more surprise for you," Jack whispered, moving his lips toward her ear.

His warm breath tickled her neck and she laughed. "Oh, really?"

Jack pulled a small box out of his pocket and opened it to reveal a diamond ring.

"Really." He got down on one knee right there on the courthouse steps. "Casey Johnson, I'm madly in love with you. Will you save me one more time, Princess? Will you marry me?"

Casey's eyes rounded. Had this handsome, wonderful man just proposed? Her heart tripled its beat. "Oh, yes!"

Her hands started trembling so badly that Jack had to grasp them and hold them still in order to put the ring on her finger. She pulled him back to his feet and snuggled up against him. "I love you, Jack. I can't imagine life without you." She gave him a kiss full of love and promise. "Are you going to be able to stand being married to a doctor?"

"Absolutely. Are you going to be able to stand being married to an FBI agent?"

"I wouldn't have it any other way," Casey answered. "God has truly blessed us."

\* \* \* \* \*

Dear Reader,

In today's society, there is human suffering all around us that takes many forms. Sometimes it is very difficult to step out of our comfort zone and help those in need, yet I am convinced that it is in these times that God uses us the most. We have to depend on Him. It's that simple.

My prayer for you, dear reader, is that you find a way to get involved in helping others. Maybe you can become a foster parent, or even an adoptive parent of a needy child. Maybe you can take meals to those dealing with sickness or loss. The choices are infinite, and with God leading your path, you can quickly become an instrument of love and compassion right in your own community.

Matthew 25:35-40 states: "'For I was hungry and you gave me food, I was thirsty and you gave me drink, I was a stranger and you welcomed me, I was naked and you clothed me, I was sick and you visited me, I was in prison and you came to me.' Then the righteous will answer him, saying, 'Lord, when did we see you hungry and feed you, or thirsty and give you drink? And when did we see you a stranger and welcome you, or naked and clothe you? And when did we see you sick or in prison and visit you?' And the King will answer them, 'Truly, I say to you, as you did it to one of the least of these my brothers, you did it to me.'"

*Kathleen Tailer*

## Questions for Discussion

1. Casey went out on a limb to help Jack, even though she knew saving Jack could have catastrophic results in her own life. Why do you think she did it? What would you have done?

2. Have you ever gone out of your way to help a friend even though it might cause problems in your own life? What was the result?

3. One of Casey's many heroic qualities was that she never broke a promise. How did that affect her relationship with others? What are Jack's best qualities?

4. Many times, Casey turned to God only when she was out of other options. What are her other flaws? What are Jack's worst flaws?

5. How did Jack's actions affect his relationship with his coworkers?

6. Casey didn't trust Jack with the story of her past. Have you ever trusted someone who let you down?

7. Do you trust God? Why or why not?

8. Casey kidnapped her niece to protect her from harm, even though it was against the law. Have you ever done something you knew was wrong and justified the action? What was the result?

9. Brett Stevens thought he was beyond hope and could never turn his life around, even with Jack's help. Was his dire outlook correct? What advice would you have given him?

10. Was it right for Casey to have to spend time in jail for her actions? Did anything good happen as a result?

11. As Casey was serving her time, what did she and Jack do to improve their relationship?

12. Do you have a relationship that needs to be mended? What is holding you back? What does God's word say to do?

13. Out of all of the characters in the book, which one do you think needed God the most?

14. What does this verse from Hebrews 13:16 mean to you? "But do not forget to do good

and to share, for with such sacrifices God is well pleased." What do you think it meant to the characters?

# *ReaderService*.com

## Manage your account online!

- Review your order history
- Manage your payments
- Update your address

*We've designed
the Harlequin® Reader Service
website just for you.*

## Enjoy all the features!

- Reader excerpts from any series
- Respond to mailings and special monthly offers
- Discover new series available to you
- Browse the Bonus Bucks catalog
- Share your feedback

*Visit us at:*
**ReaderService.com**

# REQUEST YOUR FREE BOOKS!

## 2 FREE INSPIRATIONAL NOVELS
## PLUS 2
## FREE
## MYSTERY GIFTS

*Love Inspired*®

**YES!** Please send me 2 FREE Love Inspired® novels and my 2 FREE mystery gifts (gifts are worth about $10). After receiving them, if I don't wish to receive any more books, I can return the shipping statement marked "cancel." If I don't cancel, I will receive 6 brand-new novels every month and be billed just $4.74 per book in the U.S. or $5.24 per book in Canada. That's a saving of at least 21% off the cover price. It's quite a bargain! Shipping and handling is just 50¢ per book in the U.S. and 75¢ per book in Canada.* I understand that accepting the 2 free books and gifts places me under no obligation to buy anything. I can always return a shipment and cancel at any time. Even if I never buy another book, the two free books and gifts are mine to keep forever.

105/305 IDN F47Y

| | |
|---|---|
| Name | (PLEASE PRINT) |
| Address | Apt. # |
| City | State/Prov. Zip/Postal Code |

Signature (if under 18, a parent or guardian must sign)

### Mail to the Harlequin® Reader Service:
**IN U.S.A.:** P.O. Box 1867, Buffalo, NY 14240-1867
**IN CANADA:** P.O. Box 609, Fort Erie, Ontario L2A 5X3

**Are you a subscriber to Love Inspired books
and want to receive the larger-print edition?
Call 1-800-873-8635 or visit www.ReaderService.com.**

* Terms and prices subject to change without notice. Prices do not include applicable taxes. Sales tax applicable in N.Y. Canadian residents will be charged applicable taxes. Offer not valid in Quebec. This offer is limited to one order per household. Not valid for current subscribers to Love Inspired books. All orders subject to credit approval. Credit or debit balances in a customer's account(s) may be offset by any other outstanding balance owed by or to the customer. Please allow 4 to 6 weeks for delivery. Offer available while quantities last.

**Your Privacy**—The Harlequin® Reader Service is committed to protecting your privacy. Our Privacy Policy is available online at www.ReaderService.com or upon request from the Harlequin Reader Service.

We make a portion of our mailing list available to reputable third parties that offer products we believe may interest you. If you prefer that we not exchange your name with third parties, or if you wish to clarify or modify your communication preferences, please visit us at www.ReaderService.com/consumerschoice or write to us at Harlequin Reader Service Preference Service, P.O. Box 9062, Buffalo, NY 14269. Include your complete name and address.

LI13R